THE WHITE STONE
A MYSTICAL NOVEL
FROM
EARLY IRELAND

THE WHITE STONE
A MYSTICAL NOVEL
FROM
EARLY IRELAND

ALCOTT ALLISON

COSMIC CONCEPTS Press
2531 Dover Lane, St. Joseph, MI 49085

THE WHITE STONE

A MYSTICAL NOVEL FROM EARLY IRELAND

Library of Congress Cataloging-In-Publication Data

Allison, Alcott 1958 -

The white stone; a mystical novel from early Ireland / Alcott Allison

155 pages

ISBN O-9620507-2-5 paperback; $8.95

1. Ireland--History--Fiction.   I. Title.

PS3551.L452W47   1992
813'.54--dc20   92-17296
                                                        CIP

Cover - The Christiano Design Group

Published by COSMIC CONCEPTS Press
2531 Dover Lane, St. Joseph, MI 49085

printed and bound in the United States of America

9 8 7 6 5 4 3 2 1

Type font "Meath" used for Dedication and Introduction, reminiscent of The Book of Kells, modernized by Robin Casady of Casady & Greene, Inc.

-Dedication-

For
    Those who seek
        knowing They will find

      and For

Those who will find
    not knowing
        that They seek

When Enda first met Niall, they were eleven years old. The story of their life-long friendship passed from generation to countless generations as an Irish legend of loyalty and love, similar to many another tale told not only in Ireland but in the other ancient lands. Their devotion was much more than that, as the following story tells.

This is the full, the true story of Prince Niall and his prophet Enda. Much can be learned from this history—for it is a history: although it cannot be proved to have taken place as it is written, it has been faithfully transcribed from a true source. But even if all else is overlooked, at least some who read it will wonder how many other tales of love and friendship, as well as conflict and passion, could be better understood by the discovery of what past truths lie behind them.

And remember, as you read of Niall and Enda, that none of what happened could have come to pass without the White Stone, and the greater truth that it continues to symbolize to this day.

PART ONE

The father paused. He looked down on the sleeping boy huddled in the corner farthest from the banked peat fire. He shook his head. The boy always dragged his bed as far from fire, as far from its light, as far from the rest of the family, as possible.

There was no understanding his firstborn. If you let him, he'd go three straight days without uttering one word. Then, when he did open his mouth, he was likely as not to come out with more nonsense about, "the One inside the oak tree by the byre." Of course a god was in the oak, everyone knew that—why else would Mahon have built the byre beside it, if not to gain the god's protection for the livestock? But it was for druids' sons, who would in turn become priests themselves, to talk of such things.

It was of no use to a peasant boy, who would be lucky, when he grew to manhood, to feed his family through the near-starving winters. Worse than useless, such talk could prove dangerous. The priests did not take kindly to prophets even from the royal class, just beneath their own. The king was the war-leader, but he fought when and where the priests divined.

As a poor farmer Mahon was but one step up from a slave. It had happened before now that unfortunate boys like this one had been executed for blasphemy. The gods

ordained their communication to be only through the druids and royalty. It was blasphemy—and threatening to
wealth and prestige, Mahon thought sourly—for a peasant, or even a merchant, to usurp the holy burden.

There could be no more talk about the god in the oak,
nor of the sparkling look of the wind as it swept across
the sky. The boy must do more than keep such forbidden
knowledge to himself, he must destroy his ability to feel
such things. When would he learn? Already he was eleven.
Almost grown. He must learn.

All at once exasperated, full of anger that grew partly
from love, partly from will, selfishness, fear and confusion, Mahon roughly nudged his son with his canvas-san-
daled foot. "Wake up, Enda," he said gruffly. "The sheep
are hungry, and you're still dreaming, as always."

With his father's touch and the sound of his voice,
Enda woke immediately. To his irritated father he looked
still asleep, even with his eyes open. Mahon did not know
why. To Enda the sights, sounds and smells to which he
woke every morning never lost, in that first startled moment of wakefulness, an almost ludicrous strangeness:

The roughly-cobbed walls of the small, round room,
timber covered with a mixture of clay and straw, once
whitewashed, now grimed with years of peat smoke. His
three little sisters, shrill, whining, or screaming with
laughter. The pungent odor of burning peat, the flicker-
ing glare-and-shadow rising up the wall, lunging across
the hut in the dimness as Letha, his mother, stirred the
banked fire to cook the morning meal. The minor stabbing of flattened, pithless straw against his back, sharp
ends poking through the worn cheap ticking of his mattress. The slightly sour smell of cheese, the dampness of
the mild, Irish early-morning air. The stomach-stirring
scent of smoked pig meat, and the maddening fragrance
of fresh bread, mealcakes. The greasy feeling of the
stitched sheepskins that covered him. Mahon's foot, inches
from his face, leading Enda's eyes up an expanse of leg

and trunk to his father's disapproving, impatient, and sometimes mild face.

These things, to which Mahon never gave a second thought, were brutally tangible to Enda in his first moment's return to his physical life. The shock wore off almost immediately. But in that moment Enda never failed to feel a deep inner bewilderment, a sense that these physical realities were unreal, not in the least like what he knew in his time asleep.

Enda could not actually remember what went on while he slept. But he felt, in those first few waking seconds, just as he felt the god in the byre-oak, that he had left something securely eternal for a place, this dark smoky hut, surprisingly makeshift and wobbly.

"I'm up," Enda said, rubbing his eyes and lifting himself up on his arm. "I'm coming," he added to his mother, whose back was to him as she bent near the fire, its loose hearthstones almost against the wall. Here the wall was black with soot, as was the thatch above, through which the smoke found its way out as best it could. A mouth-watering smell of mealcakes filled the room.

Letha turned as Enda spoke, almost instinctively, not first to look at her son, but to meet her husband's expected glance. Yes, she had been about to speak, to join Mahon in reproving the boy for sleeping late again. This sort of minor prophecy was usual with Enda. They could not break him of it, no matter how they tried. Some neighbors and kin had already remarked it. From here it was a short journey to the council-hall of the druids, where the matter would not be taken lightly.

Mahon worried about Enda and what would become of him. Letha carried more complicated concerns; for in addition to her trepidation for Enda, she bore a burden of guilt which she never confessed to her husband. It was her conviction that Enda received this troubling and misplaced power from her. She herself—in her youth, long before she had reached her present twenty-six years—had felt knowledge of the future press on her without welcome, perceived invisible presences which momentarily flashed into vision.

She had been grimly warned by her mother, when she was younger than Enda, to root out whatever it was in her that gave her this unwanted power; she must be rid of it lest the gods' wrath come down and destroy her. Her mother had told her the tragic story of Ceinnedi, a peasant of Connacht who had accurately prophesied a defeat in battle for his king. He had disappeared, on the night of full moon, into the sacred oak grove with the druid priests. He was seen again, but not alive, and unrecognizable except for his face, his staring eyes.

Letha, with a strength of will her husband neither suspected she possessed nor even approached possessing himself, had crushed that faculty within herself which could only bring trouble. Yet had she now passed the seed of disaster to her son, and involved the innocent Mahon as well?

Letha had never loved Mahon. This land of theirs was her dowry. Mahon, seventh of fifteen sons, was well worth such a dowry with the hope that he, like his father, might sire many sons. Nevertheless, she had come to care deeply for him, instead of hating him, as her mother had her father. Mahon was a good, kind, if simple man, who treated her well. She had expected her husband to be as careless and surly as her father, and after a short period of confusion had responded to Mahon with astonished gratitude.

It had been her sorest grief that in the twelve years of their marriage she had failed him in childbirth. The promise of his father's line was greatly fulfilled in Mahon, who had gotten six sons and three daughters on her. But of all these, only the daughters and the first son had lived for more than a few days. Five sons, stillborn or soon dead. The fault must be with her—some frailty that could not match and support the vigor of Mahon's blood.

She had another in her now, that would be born in three months' time, and she prayed to the Goddess every hour that at last there would be another healthy son. What made the sense of grief and guilt even worse for Letha was that Mahon had only once or twice reproached her, and that gently, when he was drunk, for his sadness at another infant's death.

And now, increasingly every day, Letha felt the guilt not merely of having borne Mahon an only son, but of having passed this son a taint that was, evidently, in her blood. It was possible that Mahon, for all her dowry, would never have married her had he known of the ineradicable, unpredictable, taint she carried.

"Why do the gods inflict their gift on people like us, to whom it is only a danger?" she had once asked herself, despairingly. And then, terribly frightened, she had silently pleaded for forgiveness, or at least the chance that the gods had not been listening.

Letha lowered her black eyes from Mahon's familiarly worried and annoyed blue ones, fearful that he might see her guilt in them. She busied herself removing the mealcakes from the fire, giving them to the little girls and to Mahon, with a communal bowl of raisins in the center of the circle they made on the floor. Enda came back in through the low door from the midden less than twenty feet away. The stink of it was just one more fact that Enda, now normally awake, took in his stride, as did everyone, like the reek of urine from his sisters' mattress mingling in the hut with the delicious smell of the hot mealcakes. He began to eat, hardly waiting for them to cool before cramming them into his mouth.

As if the gods had taken mercy on Letha, refusing to torment her with the constant reminder of Enda's inner resemblance to her by an equally striking outward one, the boy at eleven was very nearly a smaller version of Mahon. Letha's black eyes, greying black hair, and dark skin were repeated in two of the girls, Macha and Bebinn, but the baby, Maeve, had her father's red hair, blue eyes and fair skin. Enda still lacked a foot of Mahon's height, and his white freckled face contrasted with his father's weatherbeaten skin and red beard, but the mouth, nose, shape of the head, breadth of shoulder and sturdiness of leg were the same on each. The eyes were set the same, with the identical shade of clear blue, as blue as the Irish sky.

But there the similarity disconcertingly ended. Mahon had honest, open eyes, unpretending mirrors of his fairly simple inner workings. If one wanted to know what Mahon was feeling, one only had to look in his eyes, and see anger, laughter, or affection. Enda's eyes were also perfectly clear and open, yet one could never tell what he was thinking. What irritated people like Mahon was their unrealized awareness that Enda did not hide anything with his eyes: on the contrary, his eyes were continually reflecting the sight of something invisible to others. No one likes to feel blind, even to things that may not be there, and in Enda's presence Mahon usually felt uncomfortably blind. He loved Enda, but he knew little about him. And since Mahon knew himself to be completely normal, the inability to be known must be Enda's fault.

Mahon finished his meal and got to his feet, jerking his head to Enda. "Finish up there," he said. "I won't be coming down to the pasture today, and probably not for a long time. I've got too much to do with the other beasts and the crops, too much for one man to do in twice the time. I can't waste any more half-hours running down to you to see that you haven't lost any lambs in the brush while you've been dreaming. I need more help from you around here, and from now on the sheep are your responsibility. Anything happens to any of them, and it's you we can thank for our empty bellies when winter comes. So if you can't pay attention to what's around you for your own sake, do it for ours. Besides, from now on there'll be a beating for every mistake you make."

PART ONE

Enda scrambled to his feet, crumbs on his chin, still chewing the last huge mouthful of his breakfast. "I can watch the sheep all right," he said, replying sooner than any adult could have found possible under the circumstances. Something in his father's eye warned him not to add, "I can feel when anything's going to go wrong, and I can stop it." Why this reassurance should anger his father Enda did not know, but past experience told him it would.

"Well, do it, then," Mahon answered, but not as gruffly as he had intended. His head was stubbornly practical, but his heart was soft, and abruptly he reached out to rumple Enda's tangled, coppery hair. "I'll see you at sundown, then. Remember, don't dream all day. I'm going to teach you to braid cord soon, and then you can do that during the day, get some use out of that time you waste staring at those sheep. Letha, I'll be back for food at midday." He bent double at the low door and went out.

"Here's your bread and cheese, Enda," Letha said quietly, "and don't forget your stick and bag of pebbles. Try...." she trailed off. How could she make him see that he had to change? The story of Ceinnedi, resorted to in desperation last year, had horrified Enda, but he seemed unable to relate his own situation to that of the executed blasphemer. There was nothing more she could do. Mahon would have to solve the problem. "Go on," she said. "The dew will be off the grass before you get the sheep there, at this rate."

"Goodbye," Enda said, kissing Letha's pale, dark cheek. He looked at her a moment. She's still pretty, as old as she is, he thought. He smiled at her, pointing at her belly. "That's a boy, a strong one," he said. "Don't worry, he'll be fine." Then he bent at the door and left, letting light in as he passed from the opening.

Letha put her hands on her belly for a moment, feeling a wordless and undirected prayer. Then she picked up the baby, who was squalling, and smacked Macha and Bebinn for pinching each other.

Enda, as he drove the bleating sheep from their fold, saw his father, already small in the distance, heading for his grain fields. One quarter of the crop went to the priests, and another quarter to the king, and any yield from the livestock met the same taxes. It would almost be easier, Enda had heard the men say in the dark nights of winter, drinking strong mead around the smoking fire, to be a slave, especially of a good king like Cathal. A slave with a good master knew he would never starve, and certainly didn't have to work so hard, as they did, for so little gain.

Enda looked after Mahon, seeing more clearly at a distance than from nearby, that his back was permanently bent, though not so much as most of the other men's, even though at twenty-eight he was older than some. He didn't know what to make of Mahon, who seemed angry at his work, his life, for yielding so little. At the same time Enda sensed that Mahon never wanted anything new and different to enter his life. Except for more sons, naturally.

Enda dragged the leader of the aimless sheep to the fore and prodded him toward the pasture until he began to run. The flock, panicked at seeing their leader far ahead, began to run, but soon they all settled down to an amiable trot. Enda walked alongside, noticing little, thinking about Mahon, and Letha. They worried about so many things. In the last year or so, Enda had begun to feel in himself roilings of mingled frustration and helplessness. He was feeling that there must be something he could do, some exertion he could make, to ease their worries and satisfy them. If only he could find out what it was. After all, he loved them, and his sisters. But it was hard to know how to help them when he didn't know what had disturbed them in the first place. The byre-oak, for instance.

They acted as though no one was supposed to know the god was there, when of course everyone did. Why must they keep silent about the god? He had only mentioned it, anyway, to be saying something, when his father had angrily said, "Stop thinking all the time, it's not good for you, pay attention to what's around you, talk a little, for the god's sake." So Enda had said he'd felt the god in the byre-oak very strongly that morning. His father had looked at his mother, shaken his head, and scowled at the fire. He had not spoken again until it was time to sleep. Neither had Enda.

Enda stumbled on a stone half-covered with turf, and swore. Suddenly he felt angry too. It was stupid to pretend not to know things you knew. Why did they all do it? Not just Mahon and Letha, everyone around them knew. What was the secret reason that had everyone pretending they couldn't see the wind, or the beautiful colors round people's heads and bodies, or feel what was there and chose not to be seen?

Enda abruptly came to himself, realizing that he and the sheep had reached their grazing-pasture. He spaced the sheep on the longer grass, keeping them from the turf they had cropped the day before—too short, he realized ruefully, he hadn't been watching them closely enough. Then he crossed the pasture to his habitual resting place, a solitary oak (there was no god living in this oak, Enda knew, though how he knew he could not tell). The great tree cast its deep shade over a nearby spring, and a large, glittering white stone. He threw himself on the ground beneath the tree, resting his head comfortably on a huge, bulging root, and sighed.

It was the year 311 A.D., in Ireland where Enda was, and everywhere else for that matter, not that Enda cared. He was eleven years old; the sheep he tended clumped in creamy bundles across the green meadows and greener hills of his beloved country of Meath, and always the sun shone, either from behind the pearly-silver clouds or, as now, openly from the pure blue sky.

What did it matter the year, what had gone before or would come after, when the mild breeze lifted his heavy, red hair off his forehead and neck to cool him? The spring that welled silently into its ancient, hollowed, white stone, beneath the oak at the edge of the meadow, brought sweet water from far beneath the earth's green face, from the underground hollows where the Old Ones, the fairies, lived. (It was all right to talk around the fire about them, Enda thought cynically, as long as you never said you'd heard them or seen them.) When all that Enda needed was there for him to take, what use had he for anything so pointless as a date? The sky had not aged noticeably since Enda had been coming to the pasture, the grass and leaves always grew green again, when they were ready. The grass and trees did not obey the orders of the king, nor those of the druids, who were the ones who named, and cared about, the years. So why should Enda?

This hot feeling in the pit of his belly, this anger against being told he was wrong without having it proved to him why, was new to Enda. Without warning, it had burst into being within him and seemed to mount in his body, under his ribs, through his chest, swelling into his throat and head. It felt red, this anger, red like smoky flame from green hay burning in a summer night. It threatened to explode from his head, and suddenly Enda realized that this was what happened to Mahon when he got mad at Enda and shouted, at which time he plainly saw the muddy reddish color round his father's head. Sometimes it was hours before the usual clear green or blue color returned. That was when Enda could relax again, knowing he would not be caught unawares by a clout to his head. Such blows, Enda had found, were more painful and dizzying than those he for which he steeled himself.

18

Enda didn't like this anger and he wanted to get rid of it as soon as possible. So he deliberately took his mind from the frustrating incomprehensibility of the people in his small world, and gave his concentration to the clouds flecking the bright sky above him. From beneath the sun-spangled shade of the oak, a soft breeze trilling over and past him, the clouds seemed to travel the brilliant blue purposefully, looking down on the earth as if for something lost, soon to be found.

They were white, neat, and fluffy, and not too big, just the right kind for fooling with without making the entire sky cloudy and bringing on a shower. Enda had known ever since the time of his earliest memory that he could make clouds disappear just by looking hard at them, thinking of nothing much except what it would be like inside a cloud. The white, warm softness that would be even softer than the washed, combed fleece newly shorn from the king's sheep. He had noticed as a small boy that clouds kept vanishing, wisping away in the blue when he looked at them for a few minutes. He began concentrating to make them dissolve, and they did, very fast, very completely.

If Enda had ever spoken of this trick to his parents when he was very young, he didn't remember it. More likely, in his early childhood he had taken it so much for granted that he assumed everyone knew of it, and it was such a little thing to do that he often forgot about it for months at a stretch. When the sun poured like honey from the summer sky, and he felt too lazy to sing, or even think, he would sometimes dissolve clouds, just to be doing something. Or, now, to soothe his injured soul.

Enda, though as we have seen by the grace or curse of the gods a prophet, was a young and inexperienced one. So, as he lay on his back in the sweet clover, early morning bees buzzing industriously round him, he had no idea that coming closer to him every second was the fateful meeting of his life, the reason above all why he had been born in this place and time. One would think that the greatest things would insist on being heralded by the strongest presentiments, but often it is the reverse. When the greatest changes come to one, they are usually the last thing in the world one dreamed of.

Niall prionsa, son of King Cathal of Meath, felt an almost overpowering urge to smash his bedstead and rip its cushions to shreds. A royal rage called for some uncalculated destruction.

However, he restrained himself, because even when in high temper Niall was shrewd enough to foresee the results of such rashness. It would hardly remain a secret that he had destroyed his own bed, and then his father and all the nobles would think he had acted like a spoiled nurseling. Which, he admitted, would be true. Nevertheless, this acknowledgment, far from calming the prince, infuriated him by increasing his sense of powerlessness.

He was eleven—in less than four years he would be ready for battle, ready for marriage—yet he had never been allowed to make a single decision for himself. The only privacy he ever got was when he sealed himself in this room for hours on end. It was better than no privacy at all, but very little better. There was no freedom in his life. What Niall wanted more than anything in the world right now was to be able to ride, or walk, out into the country, into Meath his country one day, alone. Entirely alone, to see what he could find, and keep it for himself, if he liked it.

That, however, was out of the question according to every rule Niall had ever heard—and he had heard many—in his life. The prince must not be left unguarded. The prince must not venture out on his own, for danger lurked everywhere, even without reckoning those enemies of the throne who wished to harm him. The prince belonged to the nation, was the future safeguard of the realm when his father, Cathal, was in battle. Until the prince was fit to lead an army himself, he must be protected in case the king fell in battle, or died in any one of numerous ways.

The prince must not idle away his time, but study rigorously to fit himself to be a wise judge, a strong leader, a clever and fair assessor of men, a shrewd strategist. The prince must every day be drilled in weaponry, horsemanship and a swordsman's self-defense, by the best of his father's nobles. The prince must eat well, even when he did not feel like it, but he must not eat too much. The prince must learn to control his temper, and accept the responsibility the gods have given him. The prince must learn never to complain. The prince must not desire unseemly freedom, which would moreover and forever be out of his reach. The prince must realize that there remained more for him to learn than he would be able to swallow in three lifetimes, but still he must strive to master all learning, for one day he would be king. Only so, could he fitly serve the gods and the people of his kingdom. The prince, in short, bore a burden that Niall did not think worth the carrying.

He paced rapidly around his room, kicking a low stool and a wolfskin rug out of his way. The only times he'd gotten away from the palace and its grounds were the rare occasions he had been brought along on one of the nobles' long hunts, or to a feast at the palace of an ally of his father. Niall could understand why he had not been allowed to go with Cathal when he was younger, but now he could see no reason for having to stay home, like a prisoner, like a woman. If anything, it would help him see more clearly what was expected of him in the world outside the palace, to meet and be watched by all the people who were in the wider world. Yet he had been left behind.

He had not even been able to demand—respectfully, to be sure—of his father why he was not brought along. The announcement of his father's journey to a neighbor-

ing king had been made publicly, and the eyes of the
nobles had been on him to detect any sign of petulance,
of complaint, of anger. Niall had kept his face impassive,
having been brought up all his life to the necessity of protecting his inner thoughts from the impertinent scrutiny
of inferiors. But it had been hard, and in his stiffness Niall
had not even looked into his father's eyes, where, had he
done so, he would have seen understanding, strength, en-
couragement, pride and love.

That had been yesterday, and now all the men of the
court, except the old, frail ones, were gone—even his mas-
ters-at-arms. This particular visit had been so important
and stately that no one could be left behind, lest the king
of Meath appear to command a less impressive host of
nobles and warriors than his compeer. There would be no
lessons in swordsmanship for some days, only regular
practice with a serviceable substitute. His tutor, a Roman,
Plotius, captured long ago in a successful raid on the north
Welsh coast, was still at the palace, but he was addicted
to young, pretty servant girls and had indulgently, early
that morning, offered his able student a holiday.

"Holiday for him," Niall muttered scornfully after
Plotius had withdrawn. "There's nothing for me to do now
but keep shut up in here. I could read, but I'm sick of
reading. I'm sick of everything here. I want to do something."

Niall could have gone to play war-games or some
other sport with the sons of his father's nobles who lived
at court—there were a number within a year or two of
his age—but that would be more of the same princely duty
he was sick of. The other boys, and some of the girls, had
treated him as just another of themselves when they were
all younger, but in the last couple of years they had grown
conscious, as had Niall himself, that he had been born to
rule them and could never be entirely one of them.

A few of the boys were still unaffected, and most of
them were friendly, but overall things were just not the

same as they had been years ago. And the girls, too, were growing up, would be ready for marriage in another year or two, and were aware of it. They giggled now if Niall tried to talk to them, and some of them eyed him a bit warily, belying the old days of thoughtless friendship. Niall soon understood that the mothers of these girls had warned them, that since Niall had been betrothed since he was two to a princess from the West nothing good could come of any interest he might show in them. And even if unbetrothed, a prince must marry within the royal degrees. Niall had laughed on first realizing what lay behind the girls' studied coolness. The ladies of the court of Meath evidently knew little about the private education of young royals. Niall had already been told that on no account was he to approach a girl until he was twelve, and before that he would first be given into the hands of an experienced woman. If any unfortunate proof of his disobedience surfaced, such as a bastard, he would be severely punished.

Niall smiled at himself remembering that while one of the king's most stately, elderly advisors had pompously given him these instructions, he had been certain he saw the shade of a grin pass over his father's mouth and eyes. But the next moment the king had been grave again, and so was Niall, now, remembering again that on the brink of young manhood he was even less free than in his childhood. Then he had had friends, now he had none.

Niall stopped in his furious circuit of the room at the north window. He leaned against the adzed oaken sill, seduced into peace by a beautiful morning of early summer. A wild rose bramble curved, untrained, over the exterior of the window, as if it lived only to ornament his waking and drifting off to sleep. Without thinking he breathed in the lovely scent as he looked to the north.

The palace was built on a low rise, with its gardens sloping gradually to a river, beyond which ran a low drystone wall which marked the palace demesne. Beyond the wall undulated hillocks and shallow vales. The north wind blew roughly sometimes, so no crops were planted anywhere near, and the grass was too coarse for grazing. At this hour anyone in the gardens would naturally remain in the warm, southeastern demesne, just now receiving the kind waxing of the gauzy sunbeams. There was no one in sight outside the window, no one within hearing in the palace.

It seemed to Niall, as he found himself fording the river at its most shallow point, soaking his fine leather sandals as he went in to mid-thigh, that he had made no conscious decision to clamber out of his window, run down the garden slope, splash through the river, and scale the garden wall. Suddenly, he was simply doing it. He had no idea where he was headed, but the illusion of freedom he had just stolen for himself made him feel lightheaded, lighthearted on this sunny, breezy day, and he saw no reason to alter his direction once over the wall. So he continued north, sometimes running, sometimes slackening to a brisk walk. He had no idea of what he might find, but even if it was nothing, the nothing of wide, free air and vast solitude was far better than the nothing of the king's palace. Novelty is a seductive false witness to which Niall was neither first nor last to give thoughtless credence.

The spring that welled into the hollowed, white quartz stone near where Enda lay was a holy one. It had been dedicated since the beginning of time, so far as anyone knew, to a god who was never seen, but who made his presence felt in the violence of wind and storm, and in the sweetness of thick clover and grass for grazing. This was the version according to the adults Enda knew, and it had been years since he had tried to tell them where they were wrong. They not only got angry, they got frightened. All of them, Mahon and Letha included, told him

24

he must placate the god, which they believed inhabited the oak (it was no good telling them no god resided in it), by sprinkling drops of water from the spring at the base of the oak. This was to be done when he drank from the stone cup which fit a niche in the white stone, and had also been there since time immemorial. These odd instructions were just one more irritant, today, to the newly aggressive Enda. Be afraid of the gods, but pretend they're not there, he thought, half angrily, half in puzzlement. What is the matter with them?

Enda could have told them all that a far greater god than the one of the byre-oak frequented the pasture. He had long felt the occasional presence of some being, which had for its own reasons associated itself with the spring. The being was not fearsome, nor even necessarily friendly; it just was. It looked at him sometimes, and sometimes it felt to him as if it surveyed the land from sky to sky, weighing and summing up, making an appraisal Enda couldn't begin to comprehend. Nor did he especially desire to. This god was there and showed by its tolerance of Enda's presence that it didn't mind his being there. It had never occurred to Enda to try to placate a god, or curry favor with it, or keep away from it for fear of its doing harm. Up to now he had never understood the men with their sacrifices, or the women with their charms and anxious spells that almost never seemed to work anyway. He could not understand why they all seemed to want to talk to the gods, yet didn't want to admit they were all around. They were afraid, Enda thought as he lay under the oak, but why?

Enda had gone on dissolving clouds after calming himself from that unforeseen explosion of reddish anger, but he had only smoothed over his surface. As these questions came to him, without answers, the hot feeling in his belly rose again, seemed to spread through his chest, fill his lungs, speed his heartbeat. His breath came rapidly, and all at once he leaped to his feet, snatched up a hand-sized rock lying partly embedded in the turf, and threw it with all his might across the pasture. A flake of mica glinted wildly in the sun as the rock descended. It fell near a group of sheep, which scattered, bleating.

Enda stood there, panting, looking dizzily at the distant spot where the rock had fallen. For the first time in his life he was frightened, beyond the simple fear of a beating or falling from a tree he had felt when a child.

What was happening to him? He had never felt this red pain before. From one day to the next—no, not everything had changed, everything else was the same, it was only he who had changed. Once he had quietly ignored all the foolishness he met, knowing, without knowing how, that it was foolishness and accepting his instinctive awareness without thought.

This morning, anger at the world's stupidity had exploded from him without warning, concentrated on the fact that everyone showed they felt he was in the wrong! What was the point, what was the reason for knowing what others refused to admit, when they would give you no peace until you joined them in craven blindness?

Enda found he was sweating and wiped his forehead. His knees trembled a little as he sat down again, his back against the huge oak. The pounding of the blood in his ears and temples subsided, and he could hear, as he always heard when for some reason it came to his awareness, the delicate music that rang ceaselessly from and through the air. It had always made the boy happy to notice it before, but now it was like a lash on a raised welt. Mahon looked at him as if he was crazy when he talked about the music in the air, Letha looked at him sadly, with a hint of fear at the back of her eyes. The way she had looked at him this morning, when he told her the brat she carried would be a healthy son.

He sat there for a time, staring unseeingly at the sheep, the green turf, the distant hills. He never remembered what he had been thinking, because the only reason he came to consciousness then was that he felt eyes on him.

Not the routine eyes of the many presences he felt and heard in the air and the grass and the trees, and even sometimes saw from the corner of his eye for a fleeting second. This feeling was different; it was somehow more solid. He looked quickly in the direction he felt this gaze and saw a dark head duck behind a low rise to the south.

Enda, half belligerent and half afraid from what had already gone on that morning, felt in his stomach a simultaneous flash of fear and anger. If this was a thief, or a tramp who thought he was too young and weak to put up a fight, he would soon find out how wrong he was.

Enda, his dreaminess and unsettling affinity with the invisible apart, had given Mahon no cause to worry about him in mundane areas. He had always been a rough-and-tumble boy, readily joining neighboring farmers' sons, in all the rough games peasant children substituted for the knowledgeable battle-games of the young nobility. He was strong and well-grown for his age, and had fought ably, though unwillingly, when forced to. But this positive desire to fight, to have an excuse to hit something with his fist or his stick, was new to him and red like his new anger.

He jumped to his feet warily, grabbing his staff. The dark head rose to eye level and ducked again at the sight of Enda standing.

"Who is that?" Enda shouted. He began to grope inside his tunic for the whistle Mahon had given him to call for help, remembering through his aggressiveness what Mahon would do to him if anything happened to any of the sheep. The whistle's piercing note would carry over a mile on the breeze in the pure Irish air. He held it ready, but did not blow, knowing that Mahon would likely be equally angry at a false alarm.

From behind the rise the head rose a third time, followed by the well-dressed body of a boy his own age. Seeing the stranger was no larger than himself, Enda relaxed a bit, but remained on his guard. His eyes widened as he noticed the finely woven cloth of the stranger's garments, and his eyes flicked momentarily to his own coarse tunic.

Four colors he's wearing! Enda was deeply shocked at the breaking of the rules of the rigid cast society of Meath and Ireland; rules deeply ingrained in him as in any peasant or noble. If anyone reports him, they'll execute him. Only priests and poets wear five colors, and only kings wear four. And those are silver cords braided into his hair. He must have robbed a king or a prince. He must be crazy. They'll kill him, if they catch him.

Enda stood where he was, his knuckles whitening as he clutched his stick, as the insane robber came over the hillock. As he got closer Enda could see he hardly looked the part of a livestock thief. He was as tall as Enda, but slender and whippy-looking, unlike Enda who had Mahon's stocky, muscular figure. His face was more slender, too, than Enda's, with a straight aquiline nose, a long mouth, unfreckled dark skin, and large, dark eyes set under strong, silky black brows. His cheeks were lean, his forehead high, his shoulder-length dark hair neatly combed and braided with many fine, gleaming silver wires. He moved well, though cautiously now as he drew closer to this red-haired shepherd who eyed him with hostility.

"Hello," the dark boy said, confidently with just a hint of ingratiation as he looked at Enda's stick. "Are those your sheep, or are they the king's?"

"They're my father's," Enda answered coldly, "and he's within the sound of this whistle. Who are you?"

"Well, who are you?" the dark boy countered, as if a little surprised that anyone should answer him thus, or for that matter not know who he was.

"My name is Enda, son of Mahon," Enda said. "Who are you, and what do you want here? And where did you get those clothes?"

28

"My name is Niall," the boy answered, smiling as if amused at the suspicion which he now understood. "My father is Cathal, King of Meath."

This was harder to believe than that this unknown, proud-looking boy was a tramping thief. Enda laughed shortly. The anger flaming within him all that morning seemed not to respect the bounds of its own origin, but was catching and igniting everything that came within its ever-expanding reach as does real fire. This boy evidently did think him a fool.

"And what would Prince Niall be doing here in a sheep pasture, alone, away from the palace?" He had come from the direction of the capital, the king's village, Enda acknowledged in spite of his determined anger. Enda had never been there even though it was no more than an hour away on foot, but Mahon had, and he knew where it lay.

"I got away," Niall said with satisfaction. "I climbed out of my window, forded the river and got completely away without anyone knowing."

This speech made no sense at all to Enda. The boy made the palace sound like a prison, when everyone knew—as Enda had heard, all his life—there was no finer place in all Ireland. Now Enda's mind was confused. Surely no common thief would believe a palace was something to avoid. Everyone knew that life in the palace was the highest and best existence that could be attained. Another thought flashed in the shepherd's mind. This boy was possibly a prisoner being held in the palace compound who had escaped, robbing the real Prince Niall's wardrobe on his way out.

"No prince would run away," Enda said roughly. "Come on, where did you steal those clothes? And that gold torque round your neck! It must be worth twenty cattle!" Having said that, Enda realized this situation was beyond his ability to handle. He bent quickly for his whistle, which he had dropped, but the boy forestalled him as he lifted it to his mouth.

"Wait, don't call anyone!" he said urgently. "I'd have to go back right away if anyone came. I'll go back soon, but I haven't had a chance yet to see enough of the country. And as for the torque, it isn't worth more than three bullocks. It's hollow, not solid gold. It'd be too heavy to wear otherwise." He took the gold collar off and held it out to Enda encouragingly. "Here, feel."

Enda hesitated, then took the torque from Niall's outstretched fingers. Silver and copper rings, enameled, hung on several of them. He had never touched gold. "It's as warm as it looks," he said, hefting the light ornament, forgetting his suspicions for a moment at this unexpected friendliness and the novelty of the rich jewel.

"It's warm from being on me," the boy shrugged. "When you first put it on it's very cold. And I wish I had some canvas sandals like yours. These are so stiff from the river that they're chafing me."

Enda looked at Niall's gilded knee-high sandals silently. The anger was gone, or at least banked, flames muffled into embers under a soothing coat of ash.

"Well, do you believe me?" Niall asked him earnestly.

The earnestness, Enda could see, related to the fear of being sent back to wherever he had come from, and not at all to any anxiety about being treated as the prince. Those clothes, and jewels...but....

"But why would anyone run away from the palace, from being a prince?" Enda slowly asked. "You can tell everyone what to do—and no one can tell you you're wrong when you know you're right," his voice quickened as he went on. "No one can tell you not to do something." He looked from the torque in his hands to Niall and, for the first time in his life, felt a flare of envy leap within himself.

Niall laughed, rather bitterly. "That's how you think it is, eh? Well, believe me, you're a lot freer here in this pasture than I'll ever be in the palace. I asked you if you believe me. Do you, or will you blow that whistle and make me run back before anyone can get to the palace and report that I'm not there?"

It was the little things that throughout his life would carry the most weight with Enda, and the unmistakable veracity of that last remark convinced him. An additional spur to belief was Niall's accent, which Enda instinctively knew was educated, though he had never heard anyone talk that way before. Not that there was anything wrong with it: in fact, it pleased Enda without his knowing why, falling easily on ears that had heard nothing but coarse speech and the grunts of livestock. Last of the inducements to trust was the evident willingness of this boy to be friendly toward him, if Enda would let it be so. The soreness that had pained Enda all day received this silent offer of friendship as if receiving balm. The ache to be accepted as he was, for what he was, seemed eased, even if temporarily, by this boy's patent desire to stay awhile and talk to him. All right—for whatever reason he had run away from the palace, it was, Enda decided, Prince Niall himself who stood before him, and whose torque he was still holding. Hastily he handed it back.

"Yes, I believe you," he said. Suddenly he remembered hearing the men talk around the fire, at home and when his father had brought him along to visit friends, of how they had to bend the knee when they encountered the king on the road. He dropped, with the awkwardness of an unaccustomed act, on his left knee, bending his right one.

Niall did not tell him for some time that he had got it the wrong way round. In fact, what he now said was in the nature of an entreaty: "No, get up. I don't want anything to remind me of all that. I couldn't stand it any more—that's why I'm here."

He slipped the torque round his neck, as Enda got to his feet, and added nonchalantly, "I'm glad you decided to not blow that whistle. I wanted to stay here for an hour or two. It's quiet here—private. You could stay here all

31

day, without anyone watching to see if you're doing something wrong."

"Is that what they do?" Enda asked.

"Every minute of my life," Niall answered. "Except for the next couple of weeks, because all the men at court have gone with my father to visit Feredach in the South. But there's always someone to whisper to my father and the councilors whatever it is I've done wrong. Sometimes it seems as if it's everything I do...or don't do."

Enda did not know what to make of this; it was so foreign to any dreams he had indulged in about the freedom, power, and pleasures of royalty. His dreams had been fed by the tales of old women to whom he had listened when very small. In later years he had sat by the fire on long winter evenings listening to the men and an occasional traveling singer, to the tales of glorious battles and fated loves of kings. So he learned of royalty and the happenings of the court. Thus he knew that a king, a prince, had power. They gave the orders, did not take them.

It was only natural that part of Enda suspected Niall of, at best inaccuracy, at worst lying, inspired by self-pity at some just punishment received from his father. But this was only that small, carping part which is present in larger or smaller size in most of us. Almost all of Enda felt a strong, almost innate liking for Niall, now that his bad mood of the early morning had been surprised away by the prince's sudden presence. It was an odd feeling, almost as if he had known Niall for a long time. But he hadn't. This feeling of instant liking was just another of those many things Enda had never been able to explain, and had never wanted to. Until today, that is.

Enda found that he and the prince were standing uncomfortably, looking at each other, and he suggested that Niall sit under the oak. Niall agreed with some relief, telling Enda to sit also. Once they were both comfortable, the natural sensitivity in Enda told him not to start talking right away, that Niall wanted some time to adjust to where he was, how he had gotten there, and some other feelings about which Enda could not surmise. Enda was more at ease with this initial silence than most boys would have been. He had always been congenial with silence, to his father's frequent irritation. After years of suffering for the inclination, it unexpectedly came in handy.

Those feelings with which Enda sensed Niall coming to terms were both conflicting and unrelated; feelings of confusion, liberation, the oppression of knowing he must soon go back to the palace, friendship. For it was not only Enda who had felt strong, inexplicable friendliness for a stranger. From the moment the prince had come over the hillock Enda had aroused a liking in Niall, as he stood, motionless but watchful, obviously tough, with his staff at the ready.

Although Niall didn't know it, he had sensed in Enda something not to be found among any of the boys (or girls) at the palace—an intangible assurance of honesty and simplicity, an instinctive preference for the truth which is often called integrity. It unconsciously comforted Niall, this integrity in the shepherd boy, making him feel that, somehow, he had run across someone who could be trusted not only with his own ultimate, eventual adherence to the truth, but with Niall's as well. Could be trusted with it, perhaps, more than Niall himself.

No matter how strong the pressure on him, Niall felt without realizing that he did so, Enda would always stick with the truth; no matter how angry and discontented with the pain that comes with being forthright in the face of all opposition. It was more than unconscious admiration that stirred in Niall for this integrity, it was a mixed sense of joy and restfulness. Plus there was a sense that this calm honesty coming from Enda was in some way completely familiar to him, and comforting from being familiar.

Niall, naturally, did not unravel any of these mixed soul-threads at this time, nor would he for years to come. In that brief silence Enda had intuitively known he needed, he merely allowed this bubbling, unconscious awareness to calm itself sufficiently to be able to act normally again.

If Niall had been able to define his bewildering feelings that somehow made him feel both exhilarated and peaceful, he would have known why he had suddenly found himself splashing through the river at the bottom of the palace gardens, earlier that morning. He would have known, as neither boy did until much later, that destiny, when it was ready, would take any means to affect its loftily-disposed plans. Even to the extent of sending off a king and his entire court for two weeks, and providing a prince with a foolish lecher of a tutor, so that the prince might rebelliously find his way to a pasture. A pasture, distinguished only by a spring, and a white stone. One of the definite purposes of which, in its existence through untold thousands of years, was to help engender, witness, and absorb forever the spirit of the meeting which took place on that early summer morning.

Niall, having recovered from this irruption of uncomprehended coherences, soon spoke in a normal tone, with the fluency that the study of rhetoric, and his public life, had given him. "I've been looking around your pasture, Enda Mac Mahon. I like it here. It's very restful. I'd like to come here again, whenever I get the chance, if it's all right with you."

The intuitive Enda avoided any reference to Niall's right to command him if he wished, and answered the polite request like a man of dignity, though his words were boyish. "I'd be glad to have you come. It'll be good to have someone to talk to sometimes. My father yells at me because I never say anything, but I do like to talk, more than he thinks." Enda smiled briefly, thinking of what Mahon, and Letha, would say if he were ever to tell them about what had happened today.

"My father tells me I usually have too much to say, especially when it's my place to keep quiet," Niall said.

"What does your mother say?" Enda asked, remembering Letha's worn, worried face of that morning.

"Not much," Niall answered. "She's pretty busy with her women, and of course I'm busy all the time too. I used to talk to her a lot, when I was small, but in the last four or five years I've only seen her a couple of times a week, and at meals too, of course, though my father's always seated between us. And when there are royal guests, I sit farther down at the table."

Enda had not the least idea of what mealtimes were like in the vast dining-hall of a king's palace, so he was tantalized by the glimpse of royal life Niall's brief remarks gave. But he sensed that this was not the time to ask for particulars. Anyway, he was more struck by the matter-of-fact tone in which Niall spoke of seldom talking to his mother, the Banrion Cathla. He wondered how Niall could be so calm about it. Old as he was, Enda found a definite comfort in still being nearby his mother every evening, when it was dark and the fire low, or in the middle of the night, when he could hear her breathing, or was waked by the sounds and rustlings his parents made when they mated. Oh, well, it was no doubt part of the life of a prince, growing distant from your mother at an early age.

After a brief pause, Niall, making it clear he did not want to talk about his life at the palace, at least for today, asked: "What do you do here all day? Just watch the sheep?"

"I don't even do that well enough," Enda said, shaking his head at himself. "Half the time I let them wander too far, or else crop the grass right down to the roots. Sheep are the stupidest things you ever saw. They'll keep on eating in the same spot until they're eating dirt, and even then they won't stop. Most of the time I just sit here under the tree, thinking, or remembering the tales the traveling singers tell. Sometimes I sing. I know what I do a lot, I melt clouds, just for the fun of it. That's what I was doing when you came over the hill. Why don't we both work on that big one over there? I bet we can do it twice as fast together as either one of us alone."

"Melt clouds?" Niall said curiously. "What's that? I never heard of it. How do you do it?"

"You're joking," Enda said, astonished. He knew, somehow, that Niall was not afraid of the invisible gods like everyone else he knew, so he wouldn't lie about this. It must be that he really didn't know what Enda was talking about. This was very strange. If an ignorant shepherd like Enda knew about something so simple as cloud-melting, it passed all belief that an educated prince did not.

"No, I'm not joking," Niall said, a little annoyed. "What do you mean, and how do you do it?"

"I just do it," Enda said, exasperated. He and Niall looked at each other a moment, then Enda said: "Look, I'll do it now, and you watch. I'm just going to make that cloud—that one, in the west—disappear. In a minute or two. Just watch."

Niall was too polite to say anything, so he just watched Enda, and the cloud, and concealed his skepticism with that royal demeanor of his. Enda didn't seem to be doing much of anything, just looking up at the sky. The rich, checkered shade of the gently swaying oak boughs cast light and dimmer light across his fair freckled face. His red hair was struck to copper by an infiltrating ray of sunshine, and his eyes were also in the light. Oddly, though, they did not squint. They just gazed, open and as clearly blue as the sky itself, upward, without any noticeable appearance of concentration or intent.

Skepticism undiminished, even though he had liked Enda at first sight, Niall glanced up at the sky and received a profound jolt. The cloud he clearly recalled as compact and fluffy only seconds ago had broken apart in the middle and was plainly thinner and ragged at the edges. Stunned, he glanced back at Enda, who looked just as quiet and unconcerned as before, and then back at the cloud, which even in those few brief seconds had spread out much farther. It was no more than another minute before every last remnant of that firm, healthy cloud had completely vanished, leaving a temporary milky dimness on the blue western sky. Then even that was gone.

Enda had to do the same thing three more times in rapid succession before Niall could begin to credit what he had seen. "How did you do that?" he demanded, turning aside a bit, raised on one knee, so he could look directly at Enda. All thoughts of the palace, his father's journey, Plotius, the war-horses in the stables, were as far from him as the clouds Enda had dissolved. "Is it magic?"

"Of course it's not magic," Enda said impatiently. "How could I do it if it took magic? I'm only a peasant. It's the druids who know magic, and they rank even above you."

"Well then, what did you do?" Niall repeated, fascinated. This red-headed boy was the most riveting person Niall had ever met. And he didn't seem to realize in the least that he was different—good different—from everybody else.

"Nothing," Enda said, bewildered and in spite of himself annoyed. But, looking at Niall and seeing his open, obviously sincere surprise and devouring interest, his annoyance dried up. This ordinary trick of a minute or two was really utterly new to Niall. The least Enda could do was to try to help him learn more about it, since he seemed really to want.

"You must be doing something," Niall said practically, but with excitement in his voice that had long been absent. "Do you just think about it? How do you begin? Then, do you keep on doing the same thing, or do you start doing something else? Go on until the cloud disappears."

Enda shrugged. "All right." He thought for a minute or two, his face assuming the dreamy expression that aggravated Mahon. Then he began slowly: "First...I look at the cloud, concentrate on it. I watch it, and suddenly I feel as though I'm up close to it, and then I'm inside, seeing how it looks in there. Yet all the time I'm also here, looking at it from far below. When I feel myself inside the cloud, it...starts to get hotter in there. The cloud starts to get thinner, and you can see the sky behind it coming through...and then I'm down here, all of me, and as I keep concentrating on the cloud it gets thinner and drifts farther and farther apart until it's gone, into the air."

He shook his head a little, as if coming back to himself where he waited under the oak, by the spring and the white stone. He turned to Niall, who did not trouble to hide his awe and excitement but immediately began: "It is magic, I knew it was. I don't know how you've got it, but it's in you. Other people can't do this, Enda. I know I can't. I never heard of it, of anyone doing it. It's magic, and you didn't even know it!"

Enda felt the redness swirl up within him again. He did not know why, he just knew that what Niall said was wrong. It was not magic, it...it was as natural as breathing. Why did Niall, like everyone else, insist such things were magic, insist that they could not do these things? He knew they were wrong. In some way he felt free, with Niall, to stick up for what he felt to be true, instead of retreating into unplumbed silence, as he had always done. He spoke without thinking, the words seeming to flow from him in a glittering stream straight to Niall, as if the prince were their magnet and they had been formed to fly only to him and cling to him, permanently.

"It's not magic, it's something we all can do, and if we don't know we can it's only because we've forgotten. I know you can do it, I know everyone can. You just don't remember, because you were told not to, because people want to tie themselves down to only those things that they can't deny are there because they are too solid. I think people would try to pretend the entire earth wasn't here, this tree and this stone and those sheep and every ploughshare and ox if only they could get away with it. Why? Why is everyone afraid of everything around them? I don't understand. I'll never understand! You can do this cloud-melting, and you're going to do it now. You do what I said, with that little, squarish cloud over the cairn. Come on, start!"

Enda's abrupt fierceness, contrasted to the dreamy serenity that earlier had covered him like a soft white veil, made such an impact on Niall that without resistance he obeyed. He turned from those suddenly flashing blue eyes, a little nervously adjusted his back against the oak, and looked up at the cloud Enda had ordered him to dissolve.

After a few moments he felt something, some 'push', running from him up to the sky where the cloud hung, and in yet another moment he felt a small part of himself, some inner part of which he had never remembered being aware, suddenly being pulled up into the cloud. This forgotten awareness was part of him, had always belonged to him. He knew this now.

Inside the white, bluish white cloud, Niall 'saw', and yet did not see in the same way that he, down on the ground simultaneously watched the faraway cloud. As soon as he felt himself inside the cloud the temperature began to heat up, quickly, and Niall, down on the ground, noticed that the cloud thinned a little and spread slightly apart. Enda said, still in that strangely forceful voice, "See, there it goes. Just keep it hot inside there."

The cloud, much wider and thinner now with each passing second, plainly showed the blue of the sky through it as Niall abruptly felt that the part of him that had gone up to the cloud had returned. He did not detect the moment at which it had rejoined the rest of him, he only suddenly knew that it had.

"That's right, keep on watching it," Enda grinned, seeming to know every stage of the process Niall went through as he reached it.

Niall with burning concentration, a tumultuous feeling of newly awakened power and bewilderment and a touch of fear rising from his belly up to his chest, kept his eyes on the remnants of what had only three minutes before been a fat, compact, motionless cloud. In less than thirty seconds the last tattered rag of cloud had completely vanished. Hardly believing his eyes, Niall looked, blinked carefully, then looked again. There was nothing to be seen over the cairn but the deep blue, that was the Irish sky.

He looked at Enda, and as he parted his lips to speak Enda cut him off. "No, I didn't do it," he said, still in that strong voice that sounded more like the voice of a man than a boy. "I never looked at the cloud. I only looked at you. You melted that cloud. There's no other explanation of what happened to it. You melted it."

Niall stared at this shepherd with his tangled red hair, his clear blue eyes, the strong jaw that had suddenly jutted from the still-soft cheek of childhood. With the uprush of heretofore untapped energy to affect the visible with the invisible, just stirred to life in him at Enda's command, he could see the power that in this moment had made Enda so compelling. There was an iridescence all over him, like a shining spray of water. Then, as he watched, it seemed to fade away into the air around him, and Enda was suddenly just the shepherd boy again, with tranquil blue eyes and a smile as he looked at his new friend.

"I told you it was easy," Enda said, and his voice was once again the shepherd boy's, with no deep male undertone. "I told you you could do it. Everyone can do it, but most of them won't. They're afraid, I guess, but by the god of the spring and the stone, I can't tell you why."

Niall looked away, glanced involuntarily at the sky one more time to see if by chance the cloud had returned, saw it had not, and looked back at Enda. "I still don't know how it works," he said at last.

"Neither do I," said Enda. He picked up a twig and flicked a tickling insect off his lower leg with it. "And I don't care. It works, and I know it isn't anything bad that makes it work. I can feel it. When you get used to it it won't seem like anything at all. Pretty soon you'll have to watch yourself when you do it, because if you pick too big a cloud you'll make it rain for a little, or at least make the whole sky cloudy. That's happened when I've been careless."

"All right," Niall said, after another pause. "It's still hard for me to believe, but I know you're right. If you can do it, and I can do it, then probably everyone could, if only they knew how. But there's more going on here than just that. Just a minute ago you were different, you weren't like the way you are now. You were...powerful. What happened to make you like that, and why did it go away? I'm not trying to make you mad, Enda, but it did feel like magic."

It was Enda's turn to be silent. "I don't know what that was either," he said at length. "I feel the difference, too. I don't ever before remember that strange feeling coming over me, and I think I would if it had happened before. I had no idea of what I was going to say. It all just spilled out, as if somebody else was talking." He looked at Niall. "But it doesn't bother me," he added. "Whatever it was, it was something good. I'd feel if it was bad, and I wouldn't let it in."

Enda, in fact, so far from feeling bothered, was feeling glad and strong inside, as if he could climb the cairn in one jump, or run home in only a few seconds. He seemed to have gained confidence since Niall had appeared in the pasture, a sureness and relaxed bearing of himself. He laughed at Niall, suddenly, as he threw a smooth pebble at a ewe that was ambling too close to the sacred spring. "What's the matter with you?" he chuckled. "You look as if the Goddess was stalking you."

"Not the Goddess," said Niall thoughtfully, slowly. "But there's something here, something I've never before felt in my life, and I want to feel more, know more, about it. I want to come back here ten times as much now as I did before. No matter what it takes to get away, I'm going to be back here soon, and I'm going to keep coming."

Niall looked round him again, at the pasture, the white stone and the spring. He felt light inside, like a creature of air. He felt as if he had known Enda all his life. He felt as if he had been melting clouds all his life. He laughed, suddenly, and jumping up, scooped water from the spring into the stone cup and sprinkled Enda with the cold, diamond-clear essence.

Enda leapt to his feet, howling: "What was that for?"

"When you break up a cloud, you have to expect some rain," Niall shouted over his shoulder, already running. He ran fast, but Enda caught up with him, tackled him, never once considering that this was the prince of Meath whose person was sacred. They struggled, both laughing too hard to exert much strength as they sought to wrestle and pin each other to the sweet grass.

And thus it was that Niall and Enda met, and thus it was that Niall received the first of countless words of guidance from the mysterious source that chose to speak to the prince, and later the King Niall of Meath, through his prophet, Enda.

While at first the boys were able to forget their dissatisfaction there in the pasture, away from the rest of the world, this soon grew impossible. That is the way with anger, that reddish swirl, which Enda discovered on the first day with Niall: it overtakes every innocent and unrelated victim within its reach, its starting point soon lost in the black, charred waste. The more intolerable Enda and Niall found their lives away from the pasture, the tighter they bound themselves in deep sharing of their grievances and unhappiness.

Of course they did have much fun in the pasture, especially for the first couple of years after that summer morning. There were pranks, wrestling, jokes. But also it was a time of quiet talk and remembered stories, much information on life in the palace and ways of royalty and nobility new to Enda, novel anecdotes for Niall on the lives, pleasures and hardships of peasants. The boys met every fall with gloom and endured every winter only through looking forward to the spring, when the sheep would return to the pasture, and Niall could again slip away for couple of stolen hours, fooling or idling under the ancient oak by the spring and the white stone.

Niall soon taught Enda to read and write and figure, bringing a scrolled book along every now and then for Enda to devour in the pasture on those long days when Niall could not come. He also taught him war-games, which Enda liked even better. But here again, in his own way, Enda taught Niall quite as much as Niall taught him, as usual without knowing he had anything to teach.

Niall, naturally, was expected to do better at war games than anyone else ("the prince has by the grace of the gods superior ability to fit him for his tasks, but he must work always to develop and improve it"), so he was fortunate in his natural talent for fighting. He was strong and tall for his age, his eye was quick enough to allow him the utmost use of his athletic grace, and, as already stated, he had that greatest attribute of a king, a dash of coolness to settle his fiery temper.

From him Enda learned to thrust, to hang back, to sidestep, to taunt. Enda never achieved Niall's finished mastery of sword-play, but he soon learned to compensate in a typically unorthodox way. One day he astounded

Niall and surprised himself by breaking through Niall's guard, sending Niall's mock-sword spinning with one blow and pointing his own stick at Niall's throat.

"How in middle-earth did you do that?" Niall said, scowling. After all, he had not been beaten by any boys at the palace for two years, and the nobles had occasionally given him what was for them high praise. Yet Enda, with virtually no training, had defeated him.

"I don't know," Enda said lamely. "I'm as surprised as you." But seeing that Niall was about to speak, Enda quickly continued, "I know...you want me to think about everything I did and felt, in order, and tell you."

He thought for a minute, then said, still in a tone of surprise, "I guess it's pretty much like the cloud-melting. You know, you concentrate on something and suddenly you find yourself in the thing you're watching. I was concentrating on you and what you're watching. I was concentrating on you and what you'd do with the sword— the stick, I mean—and suddenly it was as if I were myself and over on your side at the same time. I knew what you meant to do and I knew what you didn't want me to do. That's when I did it."

"Let's do it again," Niall said eagerly. "If this really works, I'll be so good that for once even my father will have to tell me I'm doing well."

They began once more, and Niall, concentrating on Enda as he had on hundreds of clouds he had dissolved, almost immediately felt the 'push' of that unrecognized but familiar part of himself moving over to and surrounding his opponent. Soon, when he moved, he felt Enda's adjustment to his maneuvering as if with his own body, while remaining himself. It was as if he had two bodies, Enda's and his own, and his mind presided coolly and almost casually over both simultaneously.

After fifteen minutes Niall signaled arms-down. He and Enda each felt themselves single again as they came out of the duel. The prince found himself struck by a peculiar fact. "This is never going to work with us," he objected, "Because there's no way for one to surprise the other. No way to make the other nervous enough to strike the first blow. This can only guarantee you'll win if the other doesn't know about it. If both do, neither will strike a blow. What kind of fight is that?"

"You're right," Enda said slowly. "If everyone knew how to be with someone else and himself at the same time, there couldn't be any fights, or battles for that matter." He was silent for a moment, unsure as to what to think of this possibility. Then he shrugged and laughed. "Well, it'll be a long time before everyone knows about this, so you still can win every challenge for a long time."

So once again, in an almost unnoticed manner, Enda gave Niall something which in later years would prove to be of the utmost importance to him, and indeed to Meath, the lack of which could have led to Niall's death in battle and the changing of the history of his country. But what Niall gave Enda was in its way just as important: the opportunity to give of himself, of those qualities which seemed to both boys to be uniquely his, to the other who accepted them gladly, instead of eying him askance and rejecting what he offered.

As the years went by the boys' anger against their home situations grew stronger, even invading their quiet pasture, leaving them no refuge from the turmoil of their thoughts. There were times when each boy privately believed he must literally explode. The restrictions on their lives became increasingly intolerable, each day seeming to them the one on which no more could be borne, though somehow it always was borne to the next day, and the next. It often seemed to them as if they had nothing, nothing worth having except their secret, tacitly forbidden friendship. The one good thing they had, which the world would take from them if it could.

With this sort of furious self-absorption the order of the day, it is hardly wonderful that both boys soon forgot that voice of power which had spoken through Enda on Niall's first day near the white stone. This forgetfulness was aided by the power's lack of subsequent manifestation. Four summers had passed without its resurgence in Enda's body, without its compellingly resonant tones reaching that deep-buried core in Niall that knew to obey without hesitation.

Niall remained interested in the possession of power, but not in power's effect on him; and Enda seemed even less curious and aware of his uncommon gifts than before, in fact sometimes, briefly, seeming to regard them with animosity.

One might expect that such a state of affairs over a long period would cause the boys' friendship to deteriorate. Yet to the exact degree that each boy rebelled with mounting heat against the inexorable progress of his life, to that degree they drew closer together. Paradoxically, their love for each other strengthened as their initial envy of each other broadened and deepened over the years, in time becoming the most familiar, natural part of their friendship.

It is important to remember that the envy was only of each other's circumstances. Niall envied Enda's freedom from supervision, his license to wander the pastures and hills each day, his good fortune in being allowed to lie under the oak by the white stone during the hot, clover-scented summer afternoons, while his sheep dozed among the buzzing bees, and he drank from the stone cup, filling it again and again. He envied Enda's lack of destiny, his lack of an overriding responsibility to the people of Meath to follow a rigidly charted course which permitted no diversion and led to only one end, and that course carrying him always in the public eye.

Enda, of course, envied Niall's possession of everything Niall despised. The wealth, the luxury, the title, all that went without saying. Enda deeply desired Niall's sense of destiny, the security of knowing that whatever

he did was designed to fit him for an end which spoke
for itself as worthwhile. Niall need never worry that his
life might pass in a flash like the flutter of a dragonfly's
wing, and finish with no trace remaining of any good that
his life might have accomplished. Niall would be king; it
would be in his hands to guard Meath. And since he had
been meant for this all along, he had been given at birth
all the talents, skills and brains to fit him for this job.
There seemed to Enda a comforting neatness in the way
Niall's fate and his ability to meet it tied together with
no loose ends. But what was Enda's fate, possessed as he
was by a force both useless and dangerous to him?

And again, during all this time, where was the power
that had gleamed between Niall and Enda on their fated
meeting day? Where was the god whose presence Enda
had often felt in the pasture as a matter of course, in his
childhood? Did either boy give the spring, or the white
stone, a second thought, summer or winter, together or
apart?

PART TWO

Niall walked, deep in thought but with the restless swift stride automatic to healthy youth, in a secluded corner of the palace gardens. The gentle bright sun lit a scowl on his face and a heavy gold bracelet, set with turquoises, on his wrist.

The scowl apart, Niall, though not at the moment aware of it, or caring, made a striking figure in the peaceful landscape. He was grown, fifteen, and well-grown for his age. Tall—not so tall as his father yet, but promising such height—broadshouldered but lean withal, long-legged but sturdy, athletically graceful, promising dignity in later years.

Niall obviously overflowed with health and strength, as evident in his hot, dark eyes, as in the glow of his skin and the muscles of his arms. He was now very handsome, with braided, beaded shoulder-length hair, fine cheekbones, strong jaw, wide mouth, and narrow aquiline nose.

Those dark eyes of his, with their winglike, black brows, would have won him almost all the servant and peasant girls he had had since twelve, had he been born a slave and not a prince. The experienced woman who had been sent to his room the night of his twelfth birthday had honestly, if a little regretfully, not required him to confine himself to her for long. Her discreet report to the councilors and the king had been more than satisfactory. Of course, propriety rigidly demanded that the prince's performance in this important test be treated respectfully, with official silence, but such things had a way of leaking out.

Niall's reputation in such matters was glowingly secure, not that he cared overmuch for that either. Private satisfaction was what he had sought sexually, as in every other area of his life. This was perhaps even less possible where his sex life was concerned than in any other area, but he maintained the precious illusion by remaining obstinately deaf to female giggles and insinuations, veiled male expressions of admiration from the equally exuberant but less intelligent young nobles at the court and blind to the knowing looks of the old men, the councilors. He had already got three bastards, two on slave girls and one on a peasant's daughter. All were boys. This was the reason for the approving nods of the councilors. If Niall lived, the succession would be amply secure, if his wife bred well. That had been the problem with Niall's mother, Cathla. This son, Niall, was the only child she had conceived. The councilors were now, however, more inclined to forgiveness of her than in earlier years. The gods and the queen combined could not have given a better heir than Niall.

The scowl on Niall's face this morning derived partly from the twin questions of a wife and breeding. He had been married four months to Meta, daughter of King Airt to the West. Betrothed since Niall was two and Meta in swaddling clothes, they had not met until five days before their marriage, when Meta, her father, and a great procession had arrived in Meath with a dowry of a hundred cattle and enough gold jewels and ornaments to load onto thirty mules.

After four days of feasts, hunts, and all the rest of it, the two had stiffly endured the hours-long ceremony and feasting thereafter. That night, in Niall's bed, the poor girl, little more than a child, cried so bitterly that Niall did not touch her.

Instead, overwhelmed by the maddening realization of his powerlessness to control his own life, he had smashed into kindling the big, carved elmwood chair he had been presented with the year before. His violent rage, inexplicable to Meta, had terrified her into silence. When Niall, chest heaving and knees weak, came out of the red mist that had blinded him, he saw Meta staring at him, too frightened to close her mouth and swallow, huge green eyes in a small, white face, curly brown hair childishly drawn round her throat, as if for comfort, or ludicrous protection.

Niall was suddenly, wearily, more ashamed of having terrified this young girl than of anything he had ever done to anyone. Impossible to explain the fit of rage that had overtaken him from within. The only thing to do was to speak gently, keep his distance for little while, and try to show her that he was not, after all, a mad beast.

She finally accepted his reassurances that he was not angry with her. Nevertheless, she began to cry again, more quietly, as he came over to the bed to put one arm round her small shoulders.

At length, when her sobs had died away, he reminded her that the white linen sheet beneath them would have to be displayed next morning, by its bloodstain satisfying all that the marriage had been consummated. So Meta had submitted to what was unquestionably the most joyless act of love Niall had ever experienced. The sheet had been displayed, and all had been pleased. Meta's father, King Airt, and his train had left that very day.

Even in the act, Niall was aware of its irony, its symbolizing the invasion of his heart and mind by unyielding external pressure on this, the most intimate and deservedly private moment life offered. Perhaps this was why ancient wisdom and custom decreed early marriage for the royal heir. Should he be burdened with inconvenient sensitivities, they would avail little in opposition to the completion of the cultural demands. Even such thoughts as Niall's cannot conquer the sheer bodily vigor of fifteen. Ten years later the unthinkingly savage body may be less so, may come more under the influence of the civilized mind.

However, it was not such intimations of philosophy that brought the scowl to Niall's face this morning. It was the more mundane aspects of the situation that stung him, relentlessly, like a swarm of gadflies. In four months Niall had taken Meta only three times. After the first week or so, Meta had overcome her fear of the pain and had nightly expected Niall to roll over in bed and embrace her. He had not done so, however, until three weeks had passed, and then had seemed dispirited, though capable.

As more weeks passed with no change, Meta had nerved herself to ask Niall if something about her displeased him. "I am only thinking of the succession, my lord," she said timidly, looking at Niall's averted face. "The women are already watching me for signs of quickening. I have heard them whispering...."

"There's nothing for you to worry about," Niall told her woodenly. "Everything will happen as the gods ordain." The edge to his voice as he spoke the latter words made Meta quail, though she did not understand what it signified.

Over two months went by with no sign of pregnancy from Meta, and now she heard other whispers among her women when they thought her absorbed in her weaving or sewing. Niall did not find other women so unappealing as herself. In fact, among the girls Niall was said to be bedding daily were two of her own servants. Meta was young, but she was a king's daughter, had lived at court all her life, and knew the ways of backchat. If the gossip about Niall's dallying had spread to the women's quarters, then it was already current throughout the court.

Queen Cathla, Niall's mother, was of no help. She was a cold, reserved woman, born to the Ui Neill of the North. She showed no warmth for Meta and apparently felt little

for Niall. Even in this evil, however, there was some comfort for Meta, for Cathla was too well-bred and too uninterested to humiliate the girl with any careless commiseration on the ways of men. She saw Meta often, was polite, and made exquisite small talk, but largely kept to
her own women, who, if they gossiped either about Cathal
or Niall, did so out of the queen's presence.

Meta, an outsider at this foreign court, where she
would remain an outsider until presenting the prince with
a healthy heir, was as upset by the strangeness of her surroundings and new life as one would expect of any shy
thirteen year old girl. Now, added to the usual difficulties of royal brides, she faced this predicament which she
was completely unprepared to combat. What was wrong
with her? She must be at fault, not Niall, for according to
all reports he was constantly and energetically virile. She
must be hideously distasteful, in someway not evident
even to her modest nature, but glaringly obvious to her
lord, to cause him to shun her so.

It was the more puzzling and discouraging to her that
Niall seemed to forget occasionally that she disgusted him,
and spoke to her kindly and with some interest about herself, her activities of the day or her past at her father's
court. Then, just as she began to feel happily that this
time he might really have surmounted his aversion to her,
he would abruptly seem to recall it, and retreat into silence and absence.

Is it any wonder that the gossip circulating at court,
after four months of marriage, no quickening and Niall's
well-documented trysting, began to include rumors of the
young princess having been overheard sobbing at night
in her bed?

Niall, try as he would, was himself no longer able to
remain deaf to the gossip. His frown deepened as he
kicked viciously at the clump of daisies springing from
the green turf that was soft as a pony's nose. Whose business was it, anyway, but his own? The answer came back:

everyone's. You are the future King of Meath. You owe a royal heir to every noble and peasant under your father's rule. It is the fate of everyone that you toy with when you fail to do your duty.

This answer only made Niall angrier than he had been before during long months and years. The arrival of Meta and his permanent bondage to her was the culmination of the indignities, the deprivations of freedom, that had enraged him for years. Sex for Niall had been a happy experience till then, happy mainly because of its illusion of privacy. His sexual activity had come to represent to Niall the clutching at freedom that his inmost soul insisted it would not be denied. Not only had he chosen his partners, but he and each of them had found pleasure on universal terms that superseded those terms on which every other aspect of his life operated. Sex, to Niall, made the world outside himself irrelevant and powerless, if only temporarily. And then....

And then, malignant fate, unsatisfied with the nearly complete slavery it had imposed on him, had forced on him this political marriage, left him with no power of refusal in the matter of sleeping with this unknown girl. Stolen from him with mocking laughter the one precious bit of freedom he had managed to hide from the world and cherish. Snatched from him the one last whiff of fresh air available to him, leaving him locked in a gorgeous but grim dungeon of convention, with only stale exhalations of ancestors to breathe.

No! He would not give in on this point. If he did, he would finally be, fully and forever, a slave. It was not that Meta, in herself, was repulsive. In fact, there had been moments of thoughtlessness when Niall had felt himself rather drawn to her. She was pretty, she was sweet, there was a kind of shy pride and untested spirit in her that he sensed and admired, without knowing that he did so. But what the girl represented, made it an act of disloyalty to himself to succumb to the demands of tradition, take her cheerfully, and get as many sons on her as he could, until her fertility wore out or she died in childbirth. He would not do it, except in occasional moods of unbearable arousal when near her, and no other woman was conveniently at hand. She should be able to conceive from such moments, if she had any fire in her belly at all. But he would not give any part of himself to her, when he had not chosen her. No confidence, no friendship. Civility, no more was due from him according to his own lights.

That the civility between two who are married is necessarily widely different from that between acquaintances, was just another fact that Niall refused to admit. The struggle for inner freedom often leads one into unsuspected pettiness.

Some innate soldier's sensitivity warned Niall, as he stood, staring down unseeingly at the mutilated daisies, that he was no longer quite alone. Lifting his head sharply, he realized in another moment that the still ground was now shaking, ever so slightly, under the steps of an approaching man. Niall knew who it was. He muttered a short oath, but did not hastily swing on his heel and retreat, as he would have done on the approach of any other man.

His father came suddenly round a spinney and stopped short at the sight of Niall. "Here you are," he said in a deep voice. "I think you need to be talked to."

King Cathal was tall, broad in chest and shoulder, strong in the limbs, with the kind of heavy grace called dignity. It sat well on him. At thirty-two there were already a few threads of silver in his black hair, which glinted now in the sunlight, but which detracted little from his air of vigor. His dark eyes and striking brows were very like Niall's, as was his brown skin, but his features were heavier, if in their own way as handsome as Niall's, who had inherited his mother's patrician mien. It was well-known that Niall took after his father in more ways than one, not least of these a disinclination for peacocking.

55

Cathal had not afflicted the queen with a bedchamber visit for many years, and no one doubted that he found his full meed of pleasure elsewhere. But he made no display of his prowess, unlike many of his nobles. Niall knew this, but it had never occurred to him, in his violent self-pity, to wonder if this similarity in his and his father's demeanor hinted at deeper, emotional similarities.

Niall had always deeply loved his father. In truth, there had been no one else. Once the instinct of early childhood had been gotten over, there was no loving his mother, and he had not taken, especially, to any nurse or old Plotius the tutor, now relegated to the staff which kept the king's accounts, and still pursuing young slave girls, but careful now to confine himself to those unlikely to catch the prince's eye. No matter how admirable others in his life could have been, Niall's devotion would still have been all his father's—until he met Enda, that is. And it was about the time he met Enda, whose existence he must keep secret, that Niall's faith in his father began to waver, then, with the years, to totter. For years he had cherished the memory of a wink here, a quick grin there, when in his father's presence he had been lectured for hours on end by the druids and the councilors. In his childhood Niall had truly felt that his father understood the onerous weight he bore, sympathized, and tried to win him a little leniency, surreptitiously.

But that had begun to change about four years ago when the pressure on Niall began to mount and Cathal, evidently approving, had sat back in silence while the councilors picked holes in every action or speech of his son.

Perhaps the worst blow to Niall during all that time was the apparent, though silent, desertion of him by his father. If he had not had Enda's friendship to sustain him, the prince might not have developed into the young man the councilors complacently considered a glorious result of their wise training.

Complacently until now, that is. Niall knew with certainty why his father had sought him out this morning. He braced himself. Cathal plunged directly into the matter: "Let's walk, shall we, and we can talk about this gossip going round the court."

In spite of himself Niall felt his body stiffen visibly at his father's words, at the same time feeling his sire's quizzical gaze register the change and draw accurate and, to Niall, insufferable conclusions. Hating himself for his self-betrayal, he said nothing as he walked alongside the king.

"You've heard something of it, then, I see," Cathal said. "As I thought. Now, by the Old Ones, what's behind it? Why isn't the girl pregnant yet?"

"How should I know?" Niall flashed, forgetting himself. Then, remembering, he said: "Forgive me. But how should I know, I'm no midwife or old woman, nor even a physician. Maybe the priests can divine with their sheep's guts what all the gossips want to know. I have better things to do."

"That is another of the things I've heard," Cathal said dryly. "I understand you're even keeping some of the girls from their work in the middle of the day. But the rumors are beginning to say more than that. They say you are not only busying yourself with the slaves, you're ignoring the princess." Niall was silent, looking at the ground as they walked. Mixed in with guilt and defensiveness, a powerful fury was smoldering inside him. "Well, is this true?" the king at length asked.

Controlling himself, Niall spoke in a flat, hard voice. "I've taken her," he said. "You all saw the bloodstain the morning after the wedding, didn't you? It's not my fault she didn't get pregnant then. I've got three whelps already."

"No, you can't be faulted for the girl's failure to quicken from the wedding night," the king agreed. "But you could be faulted if in the months since then you'd barely touched her." He risked a glance at Niall, who still glared at the ground, his cheek taut from the jutting of his set jaw. He abruptly stopped walking, took Niall by the shoulders, and compelled the young man to meet his gaze. "What is wrong, Niall?" he asked gently.

Niall did not hear the gentleness. He felt only the firmness of his father's grip, the penetration of his dark eyes, the deepness of his voice. "Nothing is wrong," he said in the same hard voice. "Nothing at all." He moved away from his father's hands and started walking again.

Cathal easily kept pace with him. "Is Meta not robust enough for you?" he asked bluntly. "She's a delicate creature."

"No," Niall said shortly. Although he would avoid giving a truthful answer if he could, his loyalty to his inner cry for freedom disdained his telling an outright lie, even when it might have got him off the hook for a short time.

In any case, it would have been only a short time—if Cathal and Airt had discussed the problem, arrived at an amicable solution and return of the dowry, then Meta would have been honorably returned to her father—and then what? Betrothal to another foreign princess (and one, a suppressed part of Niall's mind insidiously whispered, probably not as pretty and sweet as the first wife fate had given him). No, if pressed to the wall, he would defiantly tell the truth, no matter what would happen to him afterward. But only if pressed to the wall.

"Forgive the question," Cathal said, "but such impediments do arise, occasionally." His voice remained sober, but Niall read in his eye the shadow of his joke and a hint of confirmation of the fact that court gossip was sometimes surprisingly detailed. Then the moment of humor was gone, and Niall had subsided into his bitter resentment again.

"What is it then?" Cathal pursued, with a glimmer of hope, now that he had reached his son for even a second.

"I didn't say there was anything," Niall reminded his father stonily. "I said there was nothing wrong."

"True," the king nodded gravely. "You were too clever for that old trap. But this is not a game, Niall. This is of great importance, this matter. I'll be plain. It is generally believed that you are not mating with your wife, and the councilors are extremely concerned. Fortunately for you, they don't know how to proceed in so delicate a matter, so I assured them that a conversation between the two of us would clear up this affair.

"Before I found you this morning, I was inclined to dismiss all the rumors. I thought it likely that some of Meta's women had heard her weeping one night while you were off fooling with one of her maids, and concocted this tale out of boredom, and some malice for Meta because she is a future queen, and supposedly has everything mortal woman could desire. But since we began this talk I have changed my mind. I think you're neglecting your wife and your duty, Niall."

With the presence of mind that would one day make a king, Niall kept silent now, when any other young man would have been too weak to not speak. His father, nothing daunted, continued.

"The question remaining is, why? Meta is a pretty little thing. She has a sweet breath and a good nature, and in spite of all that meekness I sense a good mind somewhere in that curly head. The right kind of husband could help her develop it, help her educate herself, help her become a good companion. You could have done far worse, Niall. You have a fair chance at having won a good wife in the royal marriage game."

There was no trace of self-pity, not even of wistfulness, in the king's words, although he must have been thinking of his own cold wife, still nearly a stranger to him after seventeen years. But Niall did not hear anything so subtle as the absence of a negative quality in his father's tone. All he heard was admonishment, and more exasperating than that, an apparent inability to understand what more Niall expected from life than a pretty and agreeable foreign bride.

"So," Cathal concluded, "here it is. Don't bother to deny that you hardly ever bed your wife. Allow all of us a sigh of relief at the plentiful evidence that you are capable of getting an heir on your wife if only you would bed her. Accept our bewilderment and, I am bound to say, soon our anger, at your high-handed and childish refusal to do your duty. Moreover, this is a girl with whom half the men at court would be happy to take your place. What is the matter, Niall?"

From long experience Niall recognized the note at the end of a question that meant this time his father expected a response. "If anything was the matter," he said in the light voice that fifteen thinks an effective disguise for misery, "I couldn't tell you about it in any way that could make you understand. But there is nothing wrong. I take Meta often enough to give her a chance to quicken. If I get more pleasure from bedding the girls I choose, why should anyone else care?"

"Leaving aside that bundle of half-lies," Cathal said, "there is another cause to criticize your part in all this. Your wife is unhappy in a strange land, Niall, and you are making her unhappier still. You are neither kind nor just to her, boy, and if so to her, how so to your people one day? If her timidity tries your patience, what of that? A king needs more patience and understanding than can be found among all his subjects. You know that. Yet you cruelly treat a helpless creature who in herself is nothing that could possibly provoke you. If you saw a man beating a horse or a dog, you would thrash him with your own hands until he couldn't walk."

"I would choose a dog or a horse as my own," Niall said, at the end of his self-control; pressed to the wall. "Then I would owe it good treatment. Meta was rammed down my throat by the councilors, and custom, and political alliances, and you. I didn't choose her, and I won't take her every night as if I'd wanted her above all others.

Do you know what it was like that first night?" Niall checked himself, choking back the words that spilled out of him in a hot rush. He turned away as if to run off, but Cathal grabbed him again by the shoulders and gave him a little shake. It was a shake of frustrated love, but Niall could not feel it.

"Yes, I do know," Cathal said slowly, carefully, as if speaking to a just wakened and disoriented child. "I know exactly what that was like. You forget, Niall, I was married at fifteen too, to some king's daughter that I had never met. Yet I was expected to get children on her just as if she had caught my eye with a wildflower in her hair. I'll tell you something no one else knows, except your mother. For a couple of weeks I did what you've been doing, avoided her bed because to take her seemed sordid after that love I'd had in the hay in the stables, with cook-girls and milkmaids. But I finally realized I was born to duties other men were not, and that my life must be different as a result. I accepted the fate that gods had given me, and after a time I came to have a certain peace of mind. And you have to do what I did, Niall, the sooner the better, for everyone's sake and for your own."

Niall wrenched away again from his father's grip. "If you know what it's like," he said, and he did not know there were tears in his eyes, "and you still want me to do it, then you're worse than I've ever been." He glared at his father, too desperate for freedom even to shudder at the echo of his shocking words in the air.

Anyone else in the kingdom who had spoken so to the king would have met an unpleasant end. Cathal looked at his heir, driven by the gods only knew what pressure to this defiant state, shook his head, and spoke quietly. "Niall, you will begin to treat your wife with kindness, accepting all the obligations such kindness imposes. That is all. I warn you for your own sake that you will do well if this matter is concluded, here and now. I cannot, and will not, protect you from the consequences of your persisting in this childishness." He turned and walked away with unhurried step, full in Niall's sight till he rounded the spinney by which he had found his son, and which they had left far behind in their walk.

Niall was white and trembling, partly at his own audacity in speaking so to the king, partly from uncontainable fury at what had just passed. This order! No, he would not obey it. If he did, he would lose forever any chance at freedom, at privacy, at the hope of eventual self-determination.

And now, as he spoke to himself, he remembered that there was still one more secret, one more dear thing, not yet closed off from him. Enda. The desire to see Enda rose in him so full-blown and compelling that it would have been useless to resist it, had Niall the least inclination for doing so. But he had not. There was nothing more in the world that Niall craved just now than to throw himself down on the turf beneath Enda's oak, listen to the minute sound of the spring welling into the hollowed, white stone, and simply be with Enda.

Even when they did not talk, Enda's presence was a comfort, a strengthener. Strange that Niall had never before realized that he always felt stronger after being with Enda, that in some way Enda fed him vigor and courage, though these qualities quickly dissipated when he was no more with his friend. If only, Niall felt wordlessly as he found himself fording the palace river to the north,—if only Enda and I could be near each other all the time. How much better it would be.

Even those who least suspect it, like Niall, often translate haphazard prophecies of their future into expressions of desire. Years later, when they recall their wishes, they foolishly believe that the gods have granted grace to them. But then the mind is a foolish thing, except in those people who have conquered it.

Mahon's small, round hut was four years grimier and three sons fuller than on the day Enda met Niall, the latter change satisfying Mahon beyond expression. He did not know what had changed his luck, but the whelp Letha had been carrying four years ago had been a fine, healthy boy, named Conn, and since then two more, Cormac and Diarmuid. Two of them dark and one reddish fair, but that was of minor importance to their proud father. What mattered most was that they were thriving and, even at such young ages, likely boys. Not one uncanny set of eyes in the trio, not one lisping word so far about gods, or lights in the air no one else could see. No more Endas, in short.

Letha, a bit heavier and her hair much greyer, had grown even more silent. Her husband in brief moments wondered why she showed so little joy at the blessing of sons the Goddess had finally bestowed on her, but it was not in his nature to dwell on the puzzling or depressing if these were easily sidestepped. She did her endless work efficiently, said little to anyone, and only rarely glanced at her oldest son with any naked emotion in her eyes. But on those occasions an observer would have seen some worry, some fear, and something like the emotion of a hen on hatching a raven's egg some mischievous hand had slipped into her nest.

It was unaccountable and ridiculous, but she obstinately believed that in some way Enda was responsible for the accession of sons. Ever since that morning when he had told her with strange knowledge that she carried a healthy boy, Letha had felt an indefinable change overtake her, centering in her vitals. A tingling, sparkling sensation, both invigorating and a little unnerving. It was this that she obscurely, ignorantly, but accurately connected both to Enda and the sudden flow of sons from her body. She did not know how, she did not know why, but with the starved remnant of power within her that gave a possible, partial explanation of Enda's power, she knew Enda had done something, even if he himself did not know it.

It was impossible to feel unhappy at such a blessed result as three more sons, but Letha felt a foreboding, growing in conviction each day, that one day Enda's secret would no longer be secret, that all would know him for what he was...and what then? What could fate hold for him but tragedy and death? Despite, or perhaps because of, the curse of the gods they shared, Enda was dearest to her of all her children, dearer even than the dead infants for whom she had grieved.

On this morning Letha was a little behind-hand. She gave up her morbid thoughts and turned her attention to the breakfast fire over which she was baking bread. It was still early, but Mahon had been up several hours with a sick calf in the byre, and Enda was already awake and making his morning visit to the midden.

One of them came through the low door, and it took Letha a moment, while he straightened up, to see that it was Enda and not Mahon. At fifteen Enda was more than ever like his father, of a height with him, and nearly of a breadth as well, which did not mean Enda was heavy, for Mahon was a tidy trim size, muscular but not thick. His hair was the same coppery tangle on his neck, and a beard of the same color was downy but surprisingly full on his jaw. His features, more masculine than four years ago, were good but commonplace, entirely lacking in distinction—except for his eyes. In spite of all Mahon had been able to do, in spite of Letha's silent prayers, in spite of his own angry will, Enda eyes still concealed, in their deceptively candid blueness, secrets of vision which shone forth unexpectedly when the light was right.

He sat down silently near the fire, taking a drink of water from the nearby jug, its intricately-patterned paints flaking off with age and dampness. The wetness made his lips startlingly red against his fair skin, red and full, sensuous but pressed tightly together again as he swallowed his draught. Enda's lips were usually pressed firmly together these days, an oddly eloquent sign of his unwillingness to communicate what went on inside him, even to his own consciousness.

His silence lightened, though, and his lips actually loosened into a smile as one of his brothers, the baby Diarmuid, crawled over to him eagerly, babbling. All the children were dear to him, but they all, even the little boys, seemed to feel distanced from him. Only the baby still found an uncomplicated pleasure in being near him, crowing with delight when Enda came into his sight, preferring to sleep in his lap or arms rather than in anyone's except his mother's, in the evening before all went to bed. It is inexpressible how soothed Enda's heart was each time the baby's preference made itself plain in that hut where silence, his own and his parents', made him feel a fast-grown changeling.

He scooped up the child mock-roughly in his arms, growling and pretending to toss Diarmuid up to the thatch that would soon have to be redone, so infested was it with rats. The delighted Diarmuid, losing the rudimentary coherence he had lately begun to evince, screamed wordlessly and happily. His sister Bebinn, who was braiding Macha's hair, glared at Enda, complaining: "You stir him up, Enda, and then go out with the sheep every day leaving us to keep him quiet. Can't you leave him alone?"

Enda did not answer her. He stopped tossing Diarmuid and held him close, almost as if involuntarily. He could feel the child's heartbeat against his own. After the long winter, after years of silent rebellion and the pain of loneliness, tears no longer came easily to Enda, but they were behind his dry eyes as he watched his mother cook some fish he had caught last night in a nearby river, in the long, serene Irish twilight. He had been tired enough after the long day so as to be unable to think, and he had accepted what comfort was to be had from the singing air and the plangent silence of the earth. But that comfort had not stayed with him long, had vanished as he drew near his

father's house in the deep blue of the night. The only creature in Enda's life who gave him sustained comfort, a feeling of being wanted and loved was Diarmuid. But Enda
knew this could not last. An alteration, a distancing had
come with each of the other children as they had grown,
and it would also happen with Diarmuid. Enda knew bitterly that his father only tolerated his affection for the
lad because he was still too young to be corrupted by
Enda's peculiar waywardness.

Enda, in truth, perceived more of his father's feelings
for and about him than did Mahon himself. With each
son born and surviving Mahon had, as if relieved, drawn
back a little further emotionally from his firstborn. He was
in no way suited to comprehend, or even accept, the un-
canniness in Enda, despite Enda's own apparent rejection
of it. In the last few years the young man had not once
mentioned any of the invisible things he had prattled on
about when younger, as if he now found them as repulsive as did Mahon.

But it was not enough that Enda seemed to want to
give up the power, for the more he repulsed it, the more
undeniably predominant it seemed in him to others. The
cold fact of the matter was that Mahon had transferred a
good part of his love for his first son to his succeeding
sons, who were made of plain, sturdy stuff, no moondust
mixed with their hardy clay. Mahon was a simple man
who did not want to acknowledge the existence of anything more complex than himself. He loved Enda as much
as he was able. But this was not enough for Enda, who
felt only the absence of the love that had been withdrawn.

That Enda was no longer a child but a young man
did little to decrease Mahon's uneasiness about him. In
the ordinary way of things it would naturally be considered that the time was drawing near when Enda could be
betrothed to a girl with an adequate dowry, he bringing
to the marriage perhaps a ram and a couple of ewes, a
bred cow, a littering sow. But Mahon was pessimistic as

to the chances of any such settling of his son. On the plus side was Enda's hereditary likelihood of siring many sons, his grandfather's fifteen still an impressive factor in dowry negotiations. Likewise his father's siring of nine sons in twelve pregnancies—he could not be blamed for his wife's frailty in delivering five weak or dead infants. It was obvious from looking at the sturdy youth that he had escaped any hint of his mother's physical delicacy. But Mahon counted all that insufficient, in fact, he honestly believed it would be easier on the boy had he thinner blood.

Enda had overheard him say to Letha late one night, when all were in their beds and supposedly asleep: "There's no getting round the truth that the boy's not quite normal, and you know it, Letha. And everyone else knows it, too. It's the kind of thing you can't hide forever, and it's something everyone feels about him. I don't think the poorest farmer in Ireland, with ten ugly daughters, would want to tie the ugliest to Enda. It's almost a shame he's not like some of the other unlikely lads, milkfaced and puling. I've seen him at the harvest fair and the livestock fairs, and its pretty plain he likes the girls. It's a waste of good blood, because he's not going to get a wife."

Enda did not hate his father for this speech. It hurt him, but it was clear he could not blame his father for stating what everyone knew, what he himself knew, although he fought with all his might against admitting it. He had tried, he had rigidly insulated himself from any attempts of the invisible to reach him from outside. He had refused to see and hear most of those things that in his childhood had been so naturally part of his life, his innocently joyful existence.

But with all his self-blinding, his sealing-off of the conduit to greater knowledge than sight could bring, he had not been able to convince anyone that the capricious gods had grown weary of trying to breach his defenses and had taken themselves elsewhere. Instead, it seemed appallingly plain to all that the god's wildfire rose from the deepest core of his being. It could not be kept out by any exertion when it rose within.

Recalling the silent agony of that eavesdropping night, sleepless as it had turned out to be, Enda felt the tears behind his eyes move forward intrepidly. Diarmuid grew restless in his arms and struggled away to the floor, crawling toward his noisy brothers. Though only fifteen Enda yearned for his own children, for a woman who, incredible as it would seem, would be glad to share children and a life with him.

It was the cruelest stroke of the gods that their misplaced gift should conspire to deprive him of that which he wanted more than anything. Furthermore, marriage was the only means through which his hot blood could be cooled. He was as eager for sexual love as Niall, but unlike Niall he had no gold or cattle to give a peasant girl when he left her with child, so that her parents would not only be reconciled, but glad. He could give no profit to parents for their daughter's seduction, no dowry to the girl to ensure her an advantageous marriage. A royal bastard was an honor and an economic benefit.

Niall could do this, and in addition Niall was recently married. No doubt his wife would soon present him with a child. A wife, a child, love. The tears burned in Enda's eyes, but he turned his head aside automatically and blinked, pretending it was only the smoke from the peat fire.

Niall...his friend. He hadn't seen him for many weeks, months really, and he couldn't seek him out, he must wait for the prince to come to the pasture. Yet there appeared in Enda's mind a sudden sureness that today Niall would come, that somehow he would show up to give Enda the comfort of his unfrightened friendship. Niall was too brave to be scared off, as everyone else was, by the sardonic blessing of the gods that was truly a curse. Niall had confidence and sense, and maybe Enda could borrow enough of these qualities to sustain him for a while in his lonely, hostile existence.

He knew Niall would come this morning. He hated the awareness, the Sight that told him so, but just now he was in a mood to be grateful to a demon itself for such welcome news. He jumped up, grabbed his stick and bag of stones, and bent at the low door.

"Where are you going?" asked Letha. "You haven't eaten yet, and I haven't wrapped your bread and cheese."

"I'm not hungry," Enda said brusquely, to cover the voice that told of a lump in his throat. He bent again, and ran into Mahon, just coming in from the byre. "Where off to?" he asked his son in surprise, tired but in good humor. "The calf will do now, just needs some sleep," he added to Letha. Then he returned to Enda. "You haven't eaten yet. What happens when you're starving midday? Do you kill a lamb and roast it over a fire?" He laughed as he sat down, sniffing the aroma of the sizzling fish. "Good catch last night, Enda. Stay and eat some of it."

"No," Enda said tautly. "I'm not hungry. I just want to get out of here." He ducked under the lintel before Mahon could answer. Mahon said nothing, shrugged, and began on his fish and fresh bread.

Enda got the sheep headed in the right direction, driving them at the frantic pace that he felt himself compelled to keep. He knew he would have to wait for Niall to appear, but waiting would be easier in the pasture, under the oak near the white stone and the spring, where they had always met before.

As he walked, though, he felt a wild surge of hopelessness and rage that dwarfed even the pleasant prospect of seeing Niall. What did life hold for him, at fifteen already cut off from marriage, children, love, sex, the freedom to be what he was, unmolested? It was only a matter of time before malicious, ignorant talk brought him to the council hall of the druids. That fate at least would bring to him the only grim mercy the gods would have shown him in his short life.

He felt he should look forward to the inevitable summons as a release from durance, but youth was strong in Enda and would not submit to a disappointment so comprehensive it is not really conceivable by the average man or woman. So a furious fire fought itself from all sides within him. Thus it had gone on for years. If he had not had the never-spoken but always-felt love of his secret friend Niall, Enda might not have survived his inner flames so long, with his heart and mind singed, but still intact.

Enda, the sunny-natured shepherd, what had happened to him? What could he do, where could he go, to recover himself?

Who would be foolish enough to call it coincidental that the only place he could go to now, the place of the white stone, so patiently silent all these years—was the one place on the earth where he would be able to restore himself?

Enda, after waiting two hours for Niall, was so rapt in gazing to the horizon with the blank stare of those ravaged inside, that he failed to hear Niall's approach. The prince held his hands over his friend's eyes and ordered him to submit at once. Well-trained by that same prince, Enda grabbed Niall's arms above the elbow, flipped him over, and pinned him for three seconds before Niall managed to free himself. Grinning, gulping breath, Niall said: "By the gods, it feels good to wrestle you! I love an even match more than anything. You're the only man in the world who's natural when he's with me. I'm sorry I haven't come here for so long, but I've had a lot of problems. That's why I came today—I couldn't stand it anymore, I had to be free of it for at least a little while."

Enda smiled without mirth, and his tone was so bitter that Niall, hearing it, stared. "Free of problems here? I know we used to think so. Remember what fools we used to be?"

Niall forgot about Meta, Cathal, and the councilors. "What in the name of Fir Bolgs is the matter?" he asked, jolted out of his self-pity by the pain in Enda's words. "I never heard you talk like this before. What's wrong?"

The concern in his voice was more than Enda could bear. He had fought rejection and isolation by proudly clutching those invisible chains to him, but he had no defense to kindness. Out it all poured, the loneliness, the bleak future, the rage against the gods for making him a freak and an outcast in his own world, where by rights he should be able to find what little happiness mortal life offered. But the gods made him unfit for his own world, and he belonged to no other. He could never be anything but a peasant with a power the druids claimed jealously as their own. They would see to it that he transgressed their prerogative no longer when he came to their attention. And that would probably occur before he had a chance to lay with a woman, let alone marry and have children. His life was curse, and he was powerless to change any aspect of it.

As Niall listened helplessly to this eloquent cry of grief, he was stricken with guilt. He had never realized before just how badly things stood with Enda, and he should have known. Had he not been selfishly preoccupied, fancying his own troubles the sum total of the earth, the heavens and the sea, he would have seen long before now how Enda suffered under a brutal unfairness of fate that was quite as remorseless, if not more so, than that which victimized him. Enda was in peril of his very life, and Niall only condemned to an inner slavery while living the life of greatness anyone would want. Yet, was Niall prepared to say it was not better to die at once than to live out a tedious, regimented existence? Inevitably the consideration of Enda's troubles brought Niall back to the contemplation of his own. Even among those who love as

71

deeply as these two, it is inevitable that selfishness will tarnish generous affection.

"Well," Niall said at last, when Enda had fallen silent, "you should have told me all this before. There must be something I can do, if not now, then before too long. Everything'll be all right, I promise."

"No it won't," Enda said in a hard, contemptuous voice, looking at Niall with disgust. "How stupid can you be? It's warped your mind, being a prince. You really can't believe that there are things you can't control. I don't want a prince to try to outsmart the gods and win me some false acceptance. I don't want people tolerating me but looking white-eyed behind my back, because you ordered them to let me alone. I want to be normal, to be just like everyone else, so that no one would even think of shutting me out. Can't you see that's why I hate the gods? They've done this to me, and no power of earth, not even yours, can gainsay theirs. And what's worse, even if the gods decided to grant me a little mercy now, it would be too late. They could take their Sight away from me, but not even they could make everyone forget that once I had it. It's too late for me. I'd rather die in the sacred grove than live like a two-headed calf under your protection."

Niall remained silent. He could not argue—Enda had got to the heart of the matter for both of them. But, arrogant and young as he was, he could not tolerate letting gloom overwhelm them completely. He said, shaking his head: "I guess you're right, there isn't much I can do. But," he lifted his head as if encouraged, a note of offer lightening his voice, "I can at least get you a girl before the priests get you."

Enda looked at him for a second, then burst out in a laugh heartier than he had given for weeks. "You bastard, you mean you'd actually spare me one from your herd? And what makes you think I'd take your charity?"

"You would," Niall said flatly, eying his friend critically. "You're about ready to explode for want of it."

"The expert," Enda jeered. "So, tell me, what 'problems' did you come here to get away from? Not anything to do with women, are they? Or has your new wife thrown a tantrum about your servant-girls?"

Niall's face instantly darkened. Glowering, he said: "She's about the only one who hasn't. I have no room to breathe there anymore, Enda. They won't allow me to have anything of my own. I might as well join you in Nemet, except they won't execute a royal for the same thing they'd kill you. I don't even have that way out. I'm just as trapped as you, in a different way."

Rapidly he recounted to Enda Cathal's lecture of that morning, and his own reckless repudiation of his father's authority. Enda, despite his arms-training from Niall, his secret skills of reading and writing, was still solidly a peasant. He was aghast that anyone, even the king's son, should have spoken so to the king. But he was loyal to Niall, so he said nothing about that. Instead, when Niall had finished, he asked in genuine perplexity: "But what's wrong with your wife? I know you're angry because she was pushed down your throat, like everything else. But once you got to know her, wasn't she all right? What don't you like about her?"

"That's not the point!" exploded Niall, casting round for something on which to vent his frustration; he snatched up a pebble and threw it as hard as he could. It struck the white stone and glanced off, with a sharp noise. "The point is that I won't give up the only right I've still got to all the men and all the gods who try to make me! I thought you at least would understand!"

"I do," Enda said gravely, sadly. He could see, none better, the embattled position in which Niall found himself, and from deeply intuitive knowledge of his friend's high-spirited, proud nature, he sensed the commitment to self-determination which made it seem impossible to Niall that he should back down. He, too, knew the yearning to be free with himself, unaffected and indeed unconfronted

73

by the shackles others perpetually waited to clasp on his wrists and ankles. "I do understand. But I also know it's useless to fight the gods, Niall. I've tried for years, and they've only made it harder on me. I know you can't win, and there's no sense in breaking your heart over a hopeless cause. Give in, and make the best of what you've got."

"The only thing that will break me is giving in," Niall answered grimly. "I never will, and I won't let you either—no, I won't!" he repeated imperiously, as Enda opened his mouth. "No matter how hopeless it looks to you, you can never give in. You won't be yourself anymore if you surrender, can't you see that? They can do everything to you but take away what you are inside!"

"Oh, who cares, Niall?" Enda asked wearily. "What I am inside is the only thing I hate worse than the gods who made me this way. Fight for yourself if you want to bash your head against a stone wall, but don't fight for me. There's no reason."

"I've listened to more than enough of this," a voice announced unexpectedly. "You've gone too far. Shut up and listen to some sense for a change."

Both young men almost jumped out of their skins. They whipped round toward where the voice had come from, Niall automatically reaching for his dagger. The speaker was sitting on the rim of the white stone, the lip of the hollow that held the water of the spring. He was a man of about thirty or so, tall, robust, with yellow hair and blue eyes—not bright like Enda's but dark blue, sparkling, the color of night drawing down across the sky. He smiled at them, friendly, and as if amused when they leapt to their feet and retreated a few paces, Niall with dagger drawn and Enda with his staff at the ready.

"Who are you?" Niall demanded inimically. "And how did you get here? If you were honest you wouldn't sneak up on other men." Neither boy recalled their despair of a second ago. They seized on this intruder as a welcome outlet for their fury. Yes, to their everlasting humiliation, Niall and Enda were itching for a satisfyingly violent scrum with the visitor.

"Try not to be more stupid than you are," the stranger said agreeably. "Do you think I'm really here, in the sense that you are here, encased in a thick, clay shell? If I were to let you close enough, which I won't, you could try to touch me and find nothing under your hand."

This calm query-and-assertion was not of the sort Niall was used to parrying. A tingle prickled across his scalp as he remembered where he was, and saw that the stranger was sitting on the white stone. He looked to Enda for help, but Enda was still staring at the tall man as if he were one of his damned clouds. Did Enda think the intruder would dissolve away? Very well, he would find out himself whether this man was man—or something else. He challenged: "If it's impossible to touch you, why should it matter to you if we come close? If you mean no harm, why don't you prove it?"

"Your doubts are your responsibility, not mine," the visitor said. "As to making a test of me, I won't permit it because I am not at your disposal, my lord Niall."

"How do you know me?" Niall asked sharply, still suspicious.

The man shrugged and smiled. "Doesn't everyone?"

"No," Niall said coldly.

The man regarded Niall for a moment, still smiling. Presently he suggested: "Why don't you give it up? You know who I am, and so does Enda, for all he'd rather slit his own throat than admit it. I'm the one you call the god of the spring and the stone. And, since I try to give credit where it is due, I'll add, my lord Niall, that to challenge me as you did, knowing in your heart who I am, was a sign of bravery beyond what most men are capable of. Pointless, but brave."

Enda finally tore his eyes from the stranger and met the glance Niall shot to him, as if to a lord of appeal. To

Niall, this after all was Enda's line of country. The appeal was unwillingly rejected: Enda nodded to his friend.

After the first few moments of blind aggression, Enda had known that this was no man sitting on the edge of the spring-stone. For one thing, he had no blue, green, or even red light round him, but a shimmering mantle of clear air which clung to his entire outline, reaching out as far as two feet, trembling like sheet-lightning. This, the Sight in Enda told him, did not belong to mortals.

For another thing, the very manner of Enda's awareness concerning the stranger was unique. Ordinarily, when Enda was trapped in negative emotion such as fear or anger, the Sight in him, the intuitive turning of himself to the light, was shut off from penetration to the surface of his mind. He could not, it seemed (unlike certain of the druid priests) enjoy the gift of the gods while internally turned from their light. But now Enda felt his angry obduracy overwhelmed, crushed, obliterated by the force of this stranger's presence, a light, powerful, clean and slightly uncomfortable presence, all of these shouting to the boy that here was a creature so far above and beyond the reach of his own feeble power that surrender would be wise, and in any case inevitable.

Niall, unfortunately, had not the grace of instinctive yielding that Enda had just discovered in himself. Moreover, he carried with him, as if he carried a reserve, the dross of years of anger and rebellion, which made him hardly reconcilable to any god, even one who appeared before him, addressing him with high-handed familiarity. It would be many years before caution took precedence of bravado in Niall, and then only with the long-term help of his friend, Enda.

"Well, so what?" was Niall's lamentable remark on digesting Enda's confirmation. "As far as I can see, the only thing the gods do is wreck our lives and take away every last piece of happiness they somehow overlooked. If you've come to rob us, you're too late. We've been cleaned out."

"As far as you can see?" was all the stranger said, with a laugh. It was not an encouraging sound. "And I suppose you see farther than anyone you know? Farther than your father, or his councilors, or your arms-masters, or Plotius? (Well, perhaps farther than Plotius.) And your wife? What of her? Doubtless you see farther than she. Doubtless you can understand, while she does not, what makes your treatment of her eminently sane and sensitive. Of course it is quite clear to you, though not to her, why acting toward her with what would deceptively appear to be simple human kindness, would be an intolerable invasion of your right to privacy?"

Niall was not used to mockery, and his dark face flushed darker with anger. He clutched unthinkingly at his dagger, which he had thrust back into his belt at Enda's confirmation of the god's identity. He said in a low, savage voice: "No one speaks to me like that—"

"I do," interrupted the yellow-haired man serenely. "Try to remember, in your overweening consciousness of who you are, who I am. For your own sake, not mine. I find bowing and scraping irritating, but a little humility would do wonders for you."

Enda was staring at his friend in disbelief. It hasn't sunk in yet, that's the only explanation, he thought in a dizziness of horror and wild, unbidden amusement. Urgently he grabbed Niall's shoulder, gave him a little shake, and whispered: "What's the matter with you, you idiot? You can't talk to him that way. And what do you think you're going to do with that dagger? He told you he's not really here, that if you tried to touch him you'd feel nothing."

After his shaking Niall blinked, as if unsure of himself and his surroundings, and on Enda's last words looked toward the white stone, blinked again, and peered at the stranger.

77

Enda, joining him, felt a sudden uneasy perplexity himself. The stranger had said he was not solid as they were, but he certainly looked it. His thick, yellow hair gleamed with gold and silvery glints in the warm sun; his eyes sparkled through his yellow lashes, and the sunlight brightened his skin, bringing out small, golden freckles. The cloth of his tunic—not rich, not poor—seemed thoroughly solid and wrinkled here and there. His sandals, though good, were grass-stained. He smiled again under their scrutiny, and his teeth were strong and clean.

"It's not quite true that Niall would feel nothing if he tried to touch me, Enda," said the god—for such he must be, despite his earthbound appearance, because of his intimate knowledge of them and their thoughts. "The reason I told him to not come near is that the energy level of my existence is so high that contact with it would do damage to his body, which is of low energy in comparison."

"That's what that shimmering light round you is!" Enda said quickly, without thinking that this was hardly the proper way, either, to address a god, even a god you resented.

The god, however, seemed to take less offense at Enda's honest bluntness than at Niall's royal contumely. "That's right," he grinned. "Very clever of you, especially since it's been years since you've willingly exercised your Sight. What about you, my lord Niall? Didn't you notice the light round me, and wonder what it was?"

"No," Niall said, abruptly restored to himself by the god's baiting tone. "Enda's always the one for that. I have more important things to do."

Enda looked at Niall aghast, and for a moment Niall, through his unreasoning heated resentment of the god, feared that he had gone too far. But the god was kind enough to ignore his insolence, merely taking up the conversation again from Niall's last sentence. "More important things to do? Such as rub the collective nose of the court in the fact that you will arrantly sleep with every woman in Meath except your wife, who is the only woman who has the right to expect you in her bed?"

Niall had been in a rage even before the god appeared. He had felt as if every force of god and man and earth had joined in a conspiracy to increase the pressure of the imprisonment of his spirit until either his will or his mind broke. He had resisted the titanic bearing-down, and in answer the conspirators had put a flesh-and-blood god before him, with a voice his ears could not escape and searing words his secret heart could not shut out.

But this failure on his part did not mean he would give in. It did not signify that either his spirit or his mind had been broken, would be broken, could be broken. As he had told Enda just before the god's advent, the only way his heart could be broken was if he gave up his struggle to rule himself. He would not. He would not. By all the gods themselves, he would not give up his life to them.

The anguish of his life, that had already erupted once that day, now poured out of him in a red torrent that trivialized every other cry of anguish the boys had ever heard, save for Enda's own litany of dead faith and hope. This torrent left his throat raw, his temples pounding, his fists clenched and his legs weak. And he felt, not better, not relieved, when he came to an end, but more desperate and pushed to the edge of life itself than ever before.

"Let me alone!" he cried, wildly backing off from the god and Enda alike. "Get out of here and leave me air to breathe! I know you're a god, I know you can destroy me whenever you want to. But I'd rather die now than live the way everyone wants me to. Half their rules at the palace don't make any sense, and the other half are just for the sake of crushing my spirit. They have no feeling for anything good, or private, and neither have the gods, because they all tell me that what they want me to do is what the gods want!

"Besides Enda the only good thing in my life was making love with girls I wanted to be with because I liked them and they liked me—not the prince, me, a man they wanted to bed. It may not seem like much to you, or to them, but it's all I had.

"And then Meta is dragged along with a hundred cattle, like another cow herself, to be bred to the royal bull of Meath! I am not an animal, I am a man, and you, all of you, have no right to make me follow some plan for my life that has nothing to do with my mind and my heart. I didn't choose this life, and I don't have to follow all your orders, to bring along plans of yours that I didn't make and that I don't care about. I'd rather die now than live like that.

"So, no matter what happens, I'm not going to give in to all of you and get sons on Meta when we're nothing to each other, when all we are to you and the councilors is a couple of cattle at sale in the biggest cattle-fair of all. I've done everything else you all insisted on, when I didn't want to, but I won't give in on this, because whom I love is the last bit of freedom I've got. The only good, genuine feeling in my life, except for Enda, is the way I feel with the women I choose.

"And Enda and I both know it can't last much longer, being friends like this. You should know that—even if nothing happens to me, your giving him the druids' gifts means they'll probably kill him within a year or two! If all I'm going to be able to have in a few years is that feeling I get when I'm with a girl, then do you think I'm going to give it up, even if you kill me for it?

"I didn't choose this life, and I won't do what all you want me to do, no matter what." He looked round him, and the shining pasture looked grey and lightless to him. For lightless grey is the color of willful hopelessness.

"What is all this talk about dying and being killed, my lord Niall?" the yellow-haired man said. Enda watched him closely, in fear and unclear expectation, and was relieved to see what looked like sympathy for Niall in his expression. "You have got yourself into a swivet. I don't think either one of you has realized yet that I have come into your sight and hearing so I can help you, not hurt you."

Enda lifted his head and gazed earnestly at the stranger, who was smiling again at both boys. Then he glanced at Niall, who had turned away his head, hunching his shoulder in contempt at the stranger's words. Hastily, hoping to divert the god from Niall's provoking attitude, Enda asked, sincerely withal: "But why? Help us, I mean? You've just told us we're not doing what you want us to. Why help us instead of punish us?"

"You and Niall seemed determined to meet a terrible fate," the young man said, laughing. "And let me correct one of your many false assumptions. I don't 'want' either of you to do anything. Even if I did 'want' something from you, I would have no right to ask for it or try to extort it from you. You must each make your own decisions, as we all must do."

"I have," Niall said sourly. "The only decision I can make is to refuse to take the only path I'm offered. That's my decision. A wonderful life, isn't it?"

"More of the same," the young man said reprovingly. "Do you remember, or is a few minutes ago too much of a reach for your self-indulgent little memories, the first words I said to you? I said I was tired of hearing this hogwash from you.

"Neither one of you is quite stupid enough to get away with the foolishness you've been talking these last few years. You're now at the point of consuming yourselves with your own idiocy, your own hatred of what you refuse to understand, although the truth is plain under your nose. If I did let you wreck yourselves, choke yourselves on your own bile, without trying to help you see where you've gone wrong, that would be a vengeful punishment indeed. And I am not qualified to punish anyone. In truth, there is nothing I can do but try to help you, because you have come in my way. That is the Rule: do willingly the tasks that come to you. That is why I seem to be here, as one with you—to help. And matters would proceed more smoothly if you could find it in yourself to be pleasant, my lord Niall."

Niall still refused to look at the god, who, nothing fazed, continued: "And I suggest you control that temper of yours, at least to the extent of refraining from throwing your negativity at the white stone, in the form of a pebble or anything else. You do not know what you did. Never do so again."

Niall looked up in spite of himself. The grave note of warning in the god's last words was genuine beyond all artifice. His eyes met Enda's. The result of that exchange was that Niall, meekly for him, turned to the god, and awkwardly apologized.

"Very well, let that be the end of it," the young man said casually. "Except for one thing. You and Enda are mistaken in considering me a god. If you recall, I announced myself as the one you call the god of the spring and the stone. I am no such thing."

Enda, as we have seen before, differed from Niall in being able to let go, temporarily, of preoccupation with his troubles when more urgent stimuli obtruded. Now, for the moment not the brooding young man Niall had wrestled to the turf an hour before, but the Sighted one, his bright blue eyes again reflecting the appearance of the invisible, he objected: "But—aren't you the one I've felt here for years? I know you are. I can tell by the way you feel, here, in the pasture. It's the same feeling as when you're invisible. I'm sure of it."

"You're right," the young man answered equably. "You have felt me here before, but I'm far from the only visitor to your pasture. For thousands of years many have visited this spot, and before this spot rose from the sea we frequented others, in lands far from here and lands that now, in their turn, lie beneath the sea. Sometimes we visit merely to enjoy the beauty, sometimes as movements within patterns I am not permitted to tell you about, even if you could understand. Sometimes to help people, which is why I'm here now. But the fact that we do not exist in bodies such as yours does not mean we are gods. It seems laughable to us that you ever got the idea you must worship us. It was fear, I suppose, fear of the invisible, intangible and therefore indestructible.

"You, Enda, once, several years ago, hit on that truth when you fumed here about the foolishness of the people who wanted you to pretend you did not know what you knew. Yes, I was here that day the two of you met. Who do you think it was who began to speak through Enda to you, my lord Niall, ordering you to dive into yourself and find the knowledge of how to conquer a cloud? I have been here very often during your conversations of the last four years, as I told you. Finally, I had enough. That's why I've come now, and not at some other time, to help you shape up."

Somewhere in the middle of this speech Niall came back to himself, no longer the self-blinded fool which rage had made him. For the first time he truly realized that this man was not some offensive fleshly intruder, but a mysterious being such as, for all his cloud-melting and casualness about Enda's unnerving abilities, he had never imagined he would encounter. Perhaps he and Enda were the first, the only two in all the ancient history of Ireland to be so singled out.

A god! He and Enda were speaking to, listening to, looking at, a god! That never long absent sense of power came to Niall, filling him with a flow of pride and exhilaration, laid over his deep, acidulous fury like a veil laid over the purple face of a throttled man. A god, come to help them, he said! Such an event could never have occurred in Cathal's life, nor in the councilors'.

"My lord Niall," the yellow-haired young man said with bored humor, "I've just told you I am no god, and desire no worship. Not that it matters in the end. I'll let you both in on a secret, though as you will realize when you hear it, it will be wise to keep it to yourselves. There is only one God, and at last we all come to him and to her, men and small gods and the fairies in the barrows and the woods, and all the other creatures you see and don't see who live in the light of his and her grace."

The heresy of this shocked Niall. The effect was less on Enda, who realized on hearing the young man that he had always known, somehow, that what he said was true, though he hadn't remembered the truth until it was brought to his attention. Fortunately, Niall recalled the young man's warnings about his manners, and admitted privately that it did not do to argue with a protean being, even if he claimed to not be a god. Swallowing, he confined himself to this natural question: "What do you mean, Sir, calling the god—'God', you said—'him and her'? How can that be? We know only of gods and goddesses."

"Those you speak of are others like me—some male, some female," the young man answered patiently. "We have not yet made ourselves One, even as you have not, so we are still confined to being less than all that there is. But in complete fulfillment, which is the nature of God, there can be nothing that is not all. God is both a father and a mother. How else could it be? There is only incompleteness, lack of fulfillment, when you have one without the other. You can see that truth reflected, surely, all around you. There is no milk from the cow until she is bred to the bull and has calved. A ram is only a power of frustration without a ewe. A princess must be less than the mother she truly is without a prince in her bed, willing to be a father."

This unexpected conclusion infuriated Niall. There was no respite for him, no matter how far he ran, no matter

how dearly he wanted peace. The most unlikely begin-
nings led ineluctably back to the tormenting confrontation with his unyielding fate. He had been fascinated with
the beautiful language and strong male voice of the im-
mortal young man. He had begun to hear notes of truth
within himself, strummed by words of truth. Then, sudden and stunning as a furtive blow from a leather-cov-
ered fist, came back this conspirator's pitiless insistence
on forcing him to break down, to become a spiritless creature of no will, a man so cowed that the wonder was
(Niall thought coldly) the councilors and his father should
believe he could be capable of getting children, let alone
strong sons.

All courtesy was once more forgotten. "I told you before," Niall said, his eyes like slate as he looked at the
young man, ignoring Enda, "I'm not a bull or a ram which
will rut wherever it is placed. I am a man, and I will not
breed on a woman whom my heart did not choose. I did
not choose my life, but I have tried to compromise with
custom all my life, except in this matter. Where I love
and when, is a right I cannot surrender without surrendering my will forever."

"Surrendering our will joyously is what we are here
to learn to do," the yellow-haired 'god' responded gently. "But there are many lessons ahead of you before you
reach any understanding of that one. No matter. The problem at hand is the one we must confront. Let me say, my
lord, that in the context of your faulty and partial understanding, I consider your refusal to mate like a farm animal admirable. Very few men of your youth realize that
more is due from them than instant obedience to the spur
of their desire. It is only a fine nature that can comprehend that physical love is handmaiden to a feeling of giving, and a corresponding willingness to receive and make
the two one. Enda is another who knows this truth, but
then he is another with a fine nature. It is good that to

85

the limit of your understanding you remain true to your conviction."

"But if you think Niall's right," Enda broke in, exchanging glances with his perplexed and irritated friend, "then why do you keep telling him he's wrong to not take his wife?"

"He's right as far as he sees," the young man said, "but he doesn't see very far. My lord, you feel that you are a victim of fate, of the 'gods', of custom and the councilors. You feel betrayed by your father because he expects you to do as he has done. You feel that you did not choose your life, and that therefore you have no obligation to assume the tasks your life lays before you. You feel that since there is nothing between your wife and you except political considerations, it would be a betrayal of yourself to take her as you took the peasant's daughter, for instance, giving the girl a son who will always remind her of the delight you found together. Have I stated your position fairly?"

"Yes," Niall said, a bit uncertainly, after a quick meeting of the eyes with Enda. This being, whose presence here was so extraordinary that Niall still could not quite believe in it—what was he getting at?

"Very well," the young man said, smiling yet again. "Proving you wrong in believing you did not choose your life can wait, for Enda needs that lesson as direly as you. But as to showing you your error in stubbornly insisting that you and Meta are strangers with no bond between you—behold."

On the word Niall and Enda found that with no awareness of impending change the pasture had vanished. The sheep, the stippled shade of the oak, the crystalline spring and the glittering white stone were gone. In place of the pasture there spread a wild, rocky landscape, lightless green under a lurid grey sky. A storm must be approaching, for the wind was high and whipping, hurtling the livid, great clouds across the vast, frightening expanse of heaven. The only sign of man was a hut not far from them, with a low byre attached. More frightening than this desolation and violence of nature was the inexplicable fact that they themselves seemed to be ghosts in this sudden scene.

Niall looked at Enda, who stared back at him in equal fear, yet each began to realize that the stormy wind they saw tearing at everything around them somehow left them undisturbed. Enda's red locks were stirred by no wind or even rillet of breeze; Niall's clothes fluttered not at all; no roughness of climate or weather touched their bodies, though it appeared a wretchedly cold, damp day. What had happened? Where were they, and why, and how? The two young men looked helplessly about, vainly seeking a sight of reassurance and familiarity.

"Calm down," came a familiar voice, ever so slightly tinged with derision. The boys turned in relief (so short a time ago, and they had been ready to have the bones hot from his presumed body) to the yellow-haired 'god', who was just behind them. "What's going on here?" Niall demanded. "What have you done with Enda's pasture, and why do we see this instead?"

"Enda's pasture is where it always is, in your perception of it," the god tranquilly returned. "You are what has moved elsewhere."

"That's impossible!" Niall was beginning to say scornfully, when he caught Enda's eye and remembered how much, indeed, was possible. Not only possible, in these circumstances, but probable. He swallowed his words and asked respectfully: "Where are we, and why?"

"A sign of newborn wisdom on your part, my lord," the god said approvingly. "All the other questions can wait. These two you ask are the only ones truly important at the moment. We are in the most remote reaches Connacht, one hundred and thirty years ago. No, ask no question. Just watch what there is to be seen, and listen when I choose to speak. As for why, I have already told you—to understand your mistake concerning Meta."

What could the wild tracts of Connacht, a kingdom on the far side of Ireland from Meath, a hundred and thirty years before, have to do with Niall and Meta? One hundred and thirty years! This was madness. But was not everything that had happened since Niall had arrived at the pasture that morning mad beyond all belief?

A peasant woman came out of the hut, carrying a bucket, making for a spring fifty yards distant from the miserable shelter. The boys could plainly see her drab grey hair, thick body, ragged garment, and carriage of despair. She glanced at the sky, as if afraid the coming storm was the very wrath of the gods to be visited upon her, and hurried to draw water and scuttle back to the hut.

"Let us draw closer," the god said in a detached tone, and at once they were just inside the one dreary room of the house. Niall and Enda instinctively recoiled on finding themselves in the presence of the hut's inhabitants, unable to grasp that for these people they did not exist, could not be seen, could not be touched or heard.

They glanced at the yellow-haired god, who told them: "Give over worrying. You have no more substance here, less, than the shade of the passing storm-clouds. Just watch, and learn." There was unemphasized but palpable power in his voice, and it was this that pressed Enda and Niall to overcome their disorientation and observe the scene before them.

Aside from the woman they had already seen, there was but one inmate of the house, a man of her age, also grey-haired, but thin to emaciation. He lay on a filthy pallet before a sullenly smoking peat fire, his skin sallow, the bones of his face plain beneath it. His lips were cracked and his tongue coated, his forehead dry, his dark eyes, dulled and weary, bright only with the light of fever. He was naked, covered with smelly sheepskins. The woman, kneeling beside him, took a cloth from his brow and dipped it in the bucket of water, laying it once more on his head. Then she helped him rise a little, and held a cup full of the spring water to his lips. After initial weakness he gulped thirstily, clutching at the cup to drain every drop. Then he fell back on his pallet, as if exhausted by his effort.

The grimness of what was obviously a deathbed scene was virtually lost on Niall. He was, instead of being overwhelmed by this pathetic sickbed, overwhelmed by the complete realization that somehow this peasant couple was not merely that at all. It was illogical, it was insane that the stubbornly clinging thought had ever entered his heart, but Niall knew that this woman was Meta, this man was himself.

The implications of this incredible certainty were lost on Niall for the moment. As soon as he had seen the woman and man at close quarters, he had known he was viewing his own deathbed, and the attendance of Meta at it, in some other form from what they wore now. His identification with this couple was so instant and intense that all quibbling and resistance were shut out from his consciousness. He entirely forgot the presence of Enda beside him, and of the god, until the latter spoke, and even then was only absently aware of the sound of his voice.

"Enda," the god said to him softly, "as Niall already knows, this poor man and woman are himself and Meta, alive and married in another time and place from modern Meath. Remember, now is not the time for questions. The time will come when you will ask them, and I will answer them; but not now. Remain silent, and observe."

Strange to say, Enda, with all the unused and sometimes overflowing power in him, had not shared Niall's awareness of this scene's significance. Probably the aid of personal, involuntary immersion in part of one's self, which had overtaken Niall, was necessary for any mortal caught unawares, as Enda had been. The impact of the wretchedness he saw was too great on his sensitive nature for his mind to rear up antagonistically at the god's ridiculous assertion. The heart led the mind, as in Enda it always would.

As the boys watched in fascination and compulsion deeper than they had ever felt, the dying man began to cough, hackingly but weakly—he had no strength to take breath. The woman, who had been smoothing his rough, dirty hair, cried out as if her feelings could bear to witness to his pain no longer, and grasped his hand convulsively. "Don't die, Leic! I don't want to stay here alone!"

The man's cough was almost drowned out by the pelting rain on the thatch and walls of the hut, as the sky broke. He lifted himself up again after his coughing fit had passed, and attempted to squeeze the disconsolate woman's hand. "Don't worry, Rin," he said hoarsely, grinning feebly. "I'm not planning on leaving you for a long time. When I get over this, things'll go on as they did before—for years and years." Another attack of coughing shook him, and he fell back once more on the pallet.

The tears in Rin's eyes fell down her cheeks and dropped onto Leic's hair as he lay with his eyes closed, breathing stertorously. A long, rolling thunderclap crashed in the sky above them, followed almost immediately by another. By the time the noise had died away to the steady drumming of the harsh rain, Leic's labored breathing had fallen silent. Rin, panicked, listened at his heart, opened his eyelid, then closed it again with her thumb, still holding his hand with her other hand. The dead, dry husk of the man lay on the pallet, as light and brown as a brownly pallid oak leaf in November, waiting for the wind to whisk it away.

"I only wanted to be with him," Rin sobbed, still wrapped in her coarse cloak, lying down against Leic's dead body. The inarticulate woman wept on in the near-dark of the disease-ridden hut, the black sky splitting in lightning and thunder and dim rain about her little hut on the devastated rocky moor.

At length, tired to death, she fell asleep next to her husband, still gripping his cold hand in her own.

"Here you see the nearly selfless devotion that won the two of you, now, the enjoyment of a long and prosperous life together," said the god to Niall, after a silence of untold length. "But now you would reject it, and for what reason?"

As suddenly as the boys had found themselves in Connacht, they found themselves back in Enda's pasture, under the oak. Looking around themselves again, half in shock, their disorientation was completed by the absence of the yellow-haired young man whom they had first seen sitting on the rim of the white stone.

"You will see me again," they heard the god's voice say, as if from the very air, "at a time of my choosing. Much more will be seen and understood. For now, seek to understand what you have just seen. Act. Grow. Try." Then the air felt somehow emptier, duller, and Enda knew that the 'god' had gone from the pasture and the white stone.

PART THREE

Niall, stumbling home half-unawares over the hills and grassland, could barely think. His mind was a welter of intransigent emotions and questions. Maybe he should have stayed with Enda longer to try to sort things out, but he had felt an overmastering urge to return to the palace, though why, he hardly knew. There were hours of daylight left, and he had nearly forgotten about his argument with the king that morning, so the thought that he might now be looked for was no spur.

He and Enda had remained silent for a number of minutes after hearing the invisible god's leave-taking. They did not trust themselves enough to look at the other, let alone speak. Finally, however, Enda could bear the silence no more. Bluntly he told Niall: "Now you know how I've felt all these years."

"I guess I do," Niall agreed, with relief that Enda had confirmed sharing the whole incredible experience with him. "But I don't know what to think about it."

"Better not think," Enda advised. "Whenever I've tried thinking about this kind of thing, I only feel worse and more confused."

"But I have to," Niall objected. "How can I make any sense of what's happened, of what we saw, if I don't think about what it means?"

Enda shrugged. "Maybe you're right. But in your place I wouldn't know where to begin thinking. It doesn't make any sense. How could that old peasant couple be you and your wife—a hundred and thirty years ago, in Connacht? It makes no sense any way you look at it."

"I don't know," Niall admitted slowly. "I don't know, either. But I felt it, Enda—I've never been more certain, deep inside, about anything in my life. I knew that dying man was me, and the old woman, Meta. I knew," he repeated, with helpless emphasis.

Enda regarded Niall quietly, unable to think of a single thing to say to enlighten or help him. Unable, for that matter, to settle his own soul, in which something had been deeply disturbed by the day's events. After another half hour of silence and the aimless savaging of cloverheads, Niall rose to his feet. "I've got to get back," was all he said.

Enda knew that Niall was speaking from a stronger compulsion than fear of the discovery of his absence. He felt the unmistakable ring of truth in Niall's brief sentence. He did have to get back; for what purpose it was not for Enda to inquire. He nodded, and Niall turned away toward home without another word.

Now, on his way home, Niall relived in his mind what he had seen with the god and Enda. He could picture that squalid hut on its sweeping moor so vividly—it came back to him in memory sharper, clearer, more detailed than any memory he had of being the Prince Niall. He saw Leic, and felt such identification with him that any doubts lingering as to the truth of that identification disappeared forever.

What had happened, of course, though Niall did not know it, was that the 'god' had temporarily overpowered Niall's questioning, rational surface mind. Everything Niall knew at this moment, he knew from deeply-buried inner awareness, which requires no external proof for its certainty. It was a favor from the 'god'; truly more in the nature of a blessing, to give him a taste for that inner moral certainty, so that never again would he be satisfied with anything less.

Niall saw Rin, and immediately it seemed as if some pull in his belly drew the image of Meta irresistibly to him. Without any logical progression, Niall recalled with amazing pointedness those infrequent occasions when, forgetting his injured, obstinate independence, he had talked at length with the girl, admiring her sweetness, her prettiness, her soft voice. How he had liked hearing of her life at her father's court, and her shyly-ventured but telling opinions of certain people and ways at the court of Meath. How it had seemed comfortable to talk in private with her, until he remembered she was an insinuating pawn in the political maneuvering of the councilors, and his own father. Then he had coldly turned from her, bringing—how reproachfully he saw it now—that familiar look of bewildered sadness to her face. Suddenly, again, Rin's anxious face, leaning over Leic, flashed in Niall's mind, and he felt as if he had cruelly injured a creature defenseless because she had come to him in trust.

He was not far from the palace demesne now, and he began to run, though not to the gate but to his old way of passage, the river-wall. He had no desire to see his father, or anyone else from the court, only Meta. He saw her now, clearly, as a victim of custom and politics as surely as he was himself. His disgust for the manipulation of their lives by the powerful men of both countries was as heated as ever, but he now had a new insight. What he had seen and known today made him see with the poignancy of a blinded man who, having long been without hope, suddenly regains his sight, that his retaliation against Meta for the sins of others was—well, he had no words to describe the foolishness, wickedness, asininity of it. Of himself.

Niall reached the wall, vaulted it with one hand without breaking stride, splashed across the river, and ran unseen up to his old window. He climbed in, meaning to change from his wet, dirty tunic and sandals before sending a servant to request Meta from the women's rooms into her lord's presence. He had neglected to check one of the garden sundials as he cut across the lawns, and did not know it was after four o'clock, an hour when the princess could usually be found in the royal bedchamber she shared with her husband.

Meta rose timidly from the new elmwood chair that had replaced the one Niall had broken on their wedding night. In her hands was some sewing, a cloak of Niall's. "My lord, why do you come in this way?" she began, unable to keep a quaver from her voice, both from her general unhappiness and from Niall's disheveled, intense aspect. "Is something wrong—?"

Niall was at a loss for a moment, until, looking into Meta's large green eyes, he felt again so strong a pull of recognition and union that he found himself close to her, wet and dirty as he was, his hands on her shoulders, saying gently but with an eager light on his face: "No, nothing's wrong. I just slipped on the river bank, that's all. I meant to clean up and then send for you. I want to tell you—" He stopped. Did he really mean to pour out incoherently a fabulous tale of a yellow-haired god, and a peasant couple in ancient Connacht, while trying to explain between incredulities his friendship and odd experiences with Enda the shepherd? No, it was impossible. Not forever, perhaps, but certainly for now.

He began again, plunging handsomely into as much of the truth as mattered just then. "Meta, I am sorry. I am very sorry. If I did not know you already forgive me, I would ask your pardon. I will be a better husband to you, for I have been fortunate in you without knowing it. I can only hope you will bear with such a miserable man." He took her small, fine head between his hands and gently kissed her.

Meta, poor child, would never be as sophisticated as her mother-in-law, Queen Cathla, and the other ladies of the court. When she and Niall arrived—a little late—that evening at the great hall for meat, a number of interested gossips quickly noted her glowing face, shy smile, and frequent looks of admiration at her husband and concluded that her whispered-about problem was put to rest, at least for tonight. In days to come her continued bright looks and contented air were buzzed about with satisfaction, and speculative gazes began to be cast regularly at her waist and breasts. As for Prince Niall, he certainly looked less tightly strung than in recent weeks, but there was still a grimness about him that seemed strange for a healthy, happily married prince of fifteen with everything any man could want. It was observed that he seldom spoke to the older nobles or the king, and on those occasions only with the most studied politeness. What was yet wrong with the prince of Meath?

As for Enda, he did not feel that the god's parting adjuration to "seek to understand what you have seen. Act. Grow. Try." had been meant for him. It was for Niall, as the whole marvelous visitation and transmogrification of the pasture into old Connacht had been for the prince. Who was the shepherd to rate such attention and aid from the gods as Niall Mac Cathal received? No women for Enda, no wife, no power over himself or anyone, anything else. Nothing but obscurity and helplessness forever.

Lying awake on his pallet that night, listening to the sound of his parents' mating—once comforting in childhood, now maddeningly tantalizing—Enda admitted to himself that he wanted nothing so much as to be recognized and treated as someone of importance. He wanted something like what Niall had, however Niall himself seemed to shirk it and to consider that Enda, for all his problems, was better off. He wanted to do something, while Niall seemed to think happiness lay in not being required either by circumstances or people to do anything. Except bed girls, naturally.

Although Enda had refused to think about today's experience, he was too perceptive to have missed seeing that Niall, mysteriously prompted by the god's trick, had had a change of heart toward Meta. He was probably taking her right now. Niall—Enda loved him, but why did he get everything and Enda nothing? What had Enda done, to find himself in these straits?

It was a plaint he had not stopped repeating for years and the 'god' was right, it really was past time for Enda, and for Niall, to see and understand much more.

Enda had known when he woke, one morning about two weeks later, that the 'god' was telling him that today was "the time of his choosing." He would not admit it to himself but he was eager, to see what the god would do. He had hurried through the morning routine at home, surlier than ever to everyone save for one furtive kiss for Diarmuid, and arrived at the pasture well ahead of time, to wait impatiently for Niall. The god would hardly waste his time by appearing before both of them were there, and it never crossed Enda's mind that the god had not, through this 'feeling', likewise notified Niall of his coming.

His surmise was correct, for Niall came over the low hill only ten minutes after Enda had drunk his fifth cup from the spring, at which time he had decided that Niall was too stupid to know a message when he received one, that he was not coming, and that in consequence the god himself would stay away. "Where have you been?" Enda greeted his friend truculently. "I've been here at least an hour already. You know he's coming back today."

"I know," Niall said eagerly. "I woke up just knowing it. But it was a little difficult getting away. I had to arrange some things. I only hope they don't miss me. Give me the cup, I need some water. I ran all the way."

Enda filled the stone cup at the spring and handed it to Niall, who sank gratefully on the turf, his back against the great oak. After draining the cup and refilling it, Niall observed: "This water is more bracing than mead. I've never tasted water so pure and cold. No wonder it's always been saved for the god."

"I told you I'm not a god," the resonant male voice said. "And the spring belongs to all—to God. Not only to the invisible. I can see that what I told you the other day went in one ear and out the other."

Long before this speech was over the boys had turned to the white stone to see the yellow-haired man, sitting on the spring-bowl's rim dressed as before in two colors, purple and gold, as opposed to Enda's one and Niall's four.

He smiled at them, the smile however not withdrawing the sting of his words, and added: "Listen while I explain about the spring and the white stone. I'll do it only once, so pay attention.

"This whole pasture vale is a power point, one of those many spots on the earth where the arteries and veins of the mother earth's life force cross, creating a heightened power. Underneath each of these points where the invisible lines of power meet, the Old Ones placed the white stones. The innate power of the white stones in turn drew to the spot underground domes of water. These are the source of the springs which you will very nearly always find at these power points. Most of the white stones were placed by the Old Ones some distance underground, but this white stone and spring are special.

"Those who intuitively feel the truth know this spot is particularly powerful for all that is good, but your prideful and avaricious druid priests have blinded themselves to this truth. You two have also been in the process of so doing. Over the years you have lost much of your ability to feel the power here. Childish and self-pitying. If you cannot accept the grace of being enriched by this power point, then it may as well be given to those who can. My being here is an attempt to help you see for yourselves that you would rather retain access to the white stone."

The cautionary import of the god's last words raised prickles of discomfort in the boys, but the sensation passed as he went on speaking. As on his first visit, his words and countenance plainly expressed his conviction that these two young men were among those obdurately discontented ones on whom subtlety was wasted.

"But I see no point in wasting time talking to you about what is true. You would not need such help as I can give if you were willing to understand without seeing. Very well—you shall see, and then you will think. Experience is necessary for most—you two are no different. As long as you are not so stupid as to reject the evidence of your senses, you have every opportunity of profiting by what you will see, as Niall has done, though only partially, from what he saw on the occasion of my first mission of mercy. Back in your wife's bed, are you? And moderately happy there?"

Niall flushed a little at the god's dry tone, but he managed to nod sheepishly. "And Enda, I gather, feels there was nothing for him to learn in viewing so senseless a trick played by the 'god'? That all was for the benefit of the future king of Meath? True, Enda?"

Furiously the boy wondered why he had run to this meeting. Divine visitation or not, the stranger's mockery stung his raw nerves. He might as well have spoken—the visitor needed no words to receive communication.

"I assure you," chuckled the god in tolerant pity, much as the boys would have done at the stumbling of a sleepy pup, "in God's sight a shepherd is the equal of a prince, although few men see so clearly. And for what it is worth—and that is very little, in those worldly terms which so preoccupy you—you will not long remain a shepherd. Before long you'll be known far and wide as the prince's prophet of Meath."

This magnificent prediction did not impress Enda. Coldly he stared at the ground. Niall, too, scowled once more at the thought of that gilded seat which was to him a prison. The visitor eyed them unperturbed. "But enough of this for now. The future will become the present soon enough. I want now to hear what the two of you think about what you saw with me the last time."

Enda continued to glare provokingly at the ground. Niall, anxious to avert the god's attention from his friend, lost his scowl in a puzzled frown as he groped for words that might clearly render his ghostly experience on the Connacht moor. "I don't know what it all meant," he began slowly. "But I know that somehow what I saw was Meta and me." His tone grew dogged. "I'd stake my life on it, even though there's no proof, and it doesn't make sense."

"And you, Enda?" the stranger pursued. "What do you think?"

As the god directed his intent gaze on Enda, a strange sensation came over the shepherd. A shiver ran down his spine, and suddenly he felt vacant, detached from himself. His lips parted, and the words came forth, in Enda's voice but not of Enda.

"...For it is indeed true that men live many lives, even as bulbs send forth flowers for many seasons, and from the gnarled roots of cut trees new saplings spring up. And they live, a thousand lives or one, in order to remember fully the will of God. Mistakes are made, errors are redressed, from one life to another. But always the will of God remains the still center around which the anguish and blindness they create seethes like smoke, but never so thickly as to obscure that still light. And the time will come, when God's will is at last chosen freely by all the souls of men, for men to leave the earth and sojourn among the stars. For in this world there is only separation and pain, but in the heart of God, all becomes one, and thought is usurped by love."

As he had done once before in that place, four years
ago, Enda came to himself, to find Niall eying him with
awe, as if he were not a flesh and blood man but a play-
thing for ungraspable, pitiless forces. The shepherd boy
made a hopeless gesture, slumping to the ground, like a
thing which a giant hand has dropped. Dully he repeated,
more or less to the god: "I don't want it. I don't want it."

"But you have got it," the god answered softly. "And
why? Why, Enda? Why have you, and not some other
peasant, the gift of Sight, the burden of being the voice
of the gods? Why must you, by your very nature and
against your will, bring upon yourself the vengeance of
the priests before much more time passes? What is it a
voice has just said through you. 'Mistakes are made, errors are redressed from one life to another.' Who have
you been, what have you done, Enda Mac Mahon, in a
past only your soul remembers, which makes it the will
of God that you struggle now for his sake against priva-
tion and danger?"

The two youths watched wide-eyed as the god spoke.
Confused images of mystery swam in Niall's mind, illuminated momentarily, as if by lightning, by the shock of
inescapable recognition that came back to him with the
memory of that storm-haunted hut.

How true it had been, still was for him. And even as
that 'memory' explained his marriage to Meta, so a corresponding 'memory' must exist, somewhere, somehow,
to justify the cruel plight of Enda the shepherd, blame-
less as he now appeared.

Niall was too absorbed to recollect that his own rebellion against fate must be so answered as well. He watched
Enda, white and broken, shake his head. "I don't know,"
he answered the god. "I don't care. I'm too tired to care.
I just don't care any more."

The prince was appalled, heartsick. Without realizing
how in the urgency of his present emotion he had fully
accepted the astounding import of the god's words

through Enda, he thought fiercely: Show him, for pity's sake! Show him, the way you showed me! Help him!

All prayers are answered, but unselfish prayers are answered sooner. Without a smile, with little more than indifference in his tone, the god said, somehow seeming to look deep into each boy's eyes simultaneously: "That's why I'm here."

I have sinned, Enda thought, in a churning daze of foreboding and remorse. His sight was dim, but the eyes of the god were blue and clear, seeming to drink him in as the air drinks steam.

From the hard blue sky, with a glare that hurt the eye, the sun broiled the vast waste of brown sand, windblown into ripples that gradually converged at the horizon. To the west lay a great river, its banks green and cultivated. In the near distance, a city rose, a white splendor in the blazing light. Far off, beyond the green banks and the ancient river, glinted several great structures of limestone, with walls rising inward, increasingly narrow, to meet in one peak.

In the same bodiless state they remembered from their visitation to old Connacht, the two youths looked around alertly, vigorous as if their emotions had been left behind with their sense of physical being. "Those are pyramids," Niall whispered. "We're in Egypt!"

Long ago Niall, teaching Enda as Plotius had taught him, had recounted by the white stone legends of pharaohs, barges on the great Nile, strange gods and limitless deserts. Niall's mention of the eternal land's name had stirred in Enda that sense of mysterious familiarity so common to him in boyhood, and which was such bane to him now. I know this place, he averred silently. His soul thrummed with undefined remembrance.

They found themselves in the wide portico of a great stone building without windows, standing in its own demesne outside the city. The pillars supporting the lofty roof were at least ten times a man's girth. Several doors opened into the edifice, and a number of people traversed the portico, unhurried yet with evident sense of purpose.

Their clothes were strange. The men wore gilded sandals, what looked to Enda and Niall like kilts made of cloth of gold, and, one or two of them, light cloaks held by gold brooches. In that desert heat they wore no shirts or tunics, but they were awash with jewelry: necklaces of gold plaques, headbands of gold set with gems, bracelets like coiled snakes. The women wore close-fitting dresses of cloth of gold, or robes of the softest white linen; their jewels were like the men's, except for one woman, with a pendant like a gold sunburst and a mysterious symbol in its center. All the people were dark of skin, with black hair and glowing, searching dark eyes.

A group of three ascended to the portico from the garden on the far side. There were an old woman, a young man, and the central figure, a mature man of indeterminate age and a quiet, immensely powerful bearing. As Enda saw this man, he felt the arrow of certainty which had struck Niall in old Connacht pierce through him.

There could be no quarreling, even if there was also no explanation. Beyond all doubt Enda was looking at himself, in some prior form and life. His anger was completely forgotten. He was barely aware of the god and Niall beside him. The identification with this man so overwhelmed him that he cared for nothing but his absorption.

This triad paused at the center of the portico. At this, as if responding to a signal, the other Egyptians about them withdrew behind the great bronze doors. Insubstantial, silent, Enda came closer to the group, drawn as flowing water draws a leaf into a whirlpool. Niall followed, sure from Enda's blinkless stare that he had found himself here even as Niall had found himself in Leic. Neither boy remembered the god, who watched all that passed as well as his two charges.

The tall man spoke, with the utmost of courtesy. "So then, Lido-la, and Berynius," he began, inclining his head first to the woman, then to the young man, "it comes down to this. The pharaoh Amon-Ta, who has been always a friend to our temple, is on the brink of being deposed. The Chaldean priest, Menelek, of the Temple of Earth, our enemy, is behind the scheme to anoint Amon-Ta's sister, Srateeta, as pharaoh. Menelek will assuredly destroy the Temple of Faith if he succeeds in his plans. His hatred of me, combined with his exclusion from our mysteries, fuels his enmity. He will try, once Amon-Ta is dead, to gain access to the Altar Room. And once he has failed to penetrate its secrets, he will pull down the Temple of Faith stone by stone. Cannot you see that this desecration must be prevented at all cost?"

Tall, slender, her thick silver hair flowing undressed to her waist, Lido-la shook her head. "Lord Ikhn-Om, I understand that in this world light will always be menaced by darkness; that priests will occasionally turn their eyes from heaven to earth, and cherish dreams of domination of men rather than submission to God. Yet, even acknowledging the pressure of temporal matters, I must ask: what have governments to do with the Temple of Faith? Dynasties pass, kings die. This temple enshrines eternity."

"As I know," Ikhn-Om returned. "As you know, I am High Priest of the Temple of Faith because I was born under the blue star, and the priests followed the star to my parents at their peasant farm on the river, to take and train me. In all humility, as nearly as man can do, I strive to embody the distinction between the ways of men and the way of God."

"Yet you abandon the way of faith in God's will to intrigue like any courtier, like the faithless priest Menelek himself," Lido-la said calmly.

Ikhn-Om was not a man to anger easily. Smiling reassuringly at the nervous Berynius, he countered: "Our temple cannot enshrine eternity, as you put it so well, if it is razed by evil men."

"Faith is neither protected nor confined by stone and gilding," Lido-la answered. "Should it be revealed as God's will that this monument fall, it is the part of all the defenders of faith to believe that it falls only to make way for a greater. Of course, so drastic a decision is hard for us to accept. But if we do not accept that God's will can never be subverted by men's will, we become enemies of faith, as forsaken as Menelek."

Ikhn-Om was silent, and it was evident that he had still hoped to persuade Lido-la to take his view of the matter. He looked at Berynius, and it was plain the young priest was torn between his longstanding devotion to Ikhn-Om and his conviction that Lido-la was in the right. "Berynius, you agree with Lido-la?" Ikhn-Om finally asked.

Berynius paled. "Lord, can it be right to use the powers at your disposal, the very secrets Menelek itches to possess, for worldly ends? Have you not taught me that it is a great sin to use God's power for man's will?"

"And how is Menelek to be kept from that power, except by that very power?" Ikhn-Om inquired, impatient at last. "When I invoke the mysteries of the Altar Room, I shall feel myself enacting God's will, not challenging it."

Silence again. At length Lido-la spoke. "You are determined to try to use divine gifts for kingmaking."

"No. To preserve the Temple of Faith," Ikhn-Om said, exasperated. "To what higher use could power be put?"

"Its walls may rise to the stars," Lido-la whispered, looking into the distance, "but there can be no temple where there is no faith."

"You make yourself very clear, Lido-la," Ikhn-Om said sternly. "You are excused from further attendance upon me. Berynius, what is your decision?"

Berynius, aghast, understood that the High Priest had forthwith banished Lido-la from the temple forever. He looked at her, but to his confusion found her eyes full of pity for him. His own fell as he mumbled: "I will follow you, Lord."

Lido-la regarded Ikhn-Om serenely. "I will pray for you, Ikhn-Om," she said softly. She turned, to walk down into the gardens, and then vanish from view around the corner of the temple. Her erect figure seemed to the watching Berynius as luminous as a pillar of light.

As he turned back to his mentor, the older man smiled at him. "And see who approaches," Ikhn-Om said, gesturing.

Down the road from the glittering white city surged in stately measure a retinue flaming with gold and the gemlike colors of peacock. The two priests watched until, one hundred yards from the steps of the temple, the pharaoh's litter, flanked by the royal pair of lions, was set down. A slim, youthful figure emerged, and approached the temple on foot.

"Great Pharaoh," Ikhn-Om said, inclining his head.

"High Priest of the Temple of Faith, I come to you in all humility," Amon-Ta responded.

"It is God alone before whom you bow your head," Ikhn-Om finished the ceremonial greeting.

The pharaoh turned and signaled to his retinue. With surprise Berynius saw the host turn and retreat along the ribbon of white pavement toward the city.

Amon-Ta swung back to the priests. "There can be no going back," he said rapidly, his lean face tense, his black eyes shining with fear and determination. He was sixteen years old. "I am sure my assassination was planned for today. By now Menelek and Srateeta doubtless know I am gone, and where."

"I see," Ikhn-Om replied, as if deep in thought.

"Your temple has always had my favor, as you know, Lord," Amon-Ta continued. "If in this crisis you will exert yourself with those gifts all Egypt knows you to possess, I promise my protection until I die."

Gravely Ikhn-Om said, "What is it you believe ought to be done?"

"Menelek must be struck down," Amon-Ta said resolutely. "And, though I regret it, my sister Srateeta also. Even with Menelek dead, there will always be danger of another schemer succeeding while she lives. Yet how can Menelek be reached, and Srateeta while with him, except by such power as yours? Soldiers and courtiers have been too afraid of his dark arts even to attempt his assassination. You, Lord Ikhn-Om, must intervene. For if I fall at Menelek's hands, the Temple of Faith will fall too. And that," he added with what he imagined to be cunning, "you must not permit."

Berynius, horrified and disdainful of what the pharaoh proposed regarding his sister, and even Menelek, looked to Ikhn-Om. The high priest stood motionless for a time. Then, abruptly, he lifted his head and ordered curtly: "Come."

On entering the temple, Ikhn-Om led Amon-Ta and Berynius through a bewildering maze of passages and stairs. The sweating, desperate pharaoh was completely disoriented by the time Ikhn-Om paused before a small door, worked entirely of silver. A diffuse illumination, here as throughout the windowless temple, enabled them to see the intricate marvels cast into the metal. So perfectly designed was the temple that not only was the dim golden light evenly pervasive, but everywhere tiny currents of air swept the atmosphere perpetually fresh and clean.

Ikhn-Om turned to his companions. "Beyond this door lies the Altar Room of the Temple of Faith. Within repose the mysteries of the Unknowable God. Seek not, Pharaoh, to understand. Instead submit to the awe of your soul when you enter, the first living creature not a priest to do so in the untold years this temple has stood."

Amon-Ta, already pulled as taut as a harp string, swallowed and nodded. Ignoring him, Ikhn-Om then passed his hands over a boss upon the upper left quadrant of the door, in a series of arcane gestures. The door opened, slowly, silently. Ikhn-Om entered; Berynius, putting his finger to his lips warningly, ushered the pharaoh before him.

Amon-Ta cautiously looked around, seeing a high room built of great blocks of polished brown stone. An enormous tapestry, the color of midnight, embroidered in gold, hung high on one wall. Other, smaller hangings adorned the chamber as well. Statues rested upon pillars, and great discs of gold were suspended from the shadowy ceiling. As with the rest of the temple, the chamber was illuminated by a vague, swimming light; but, oddly, it was much brighter, a pure white, in the center of the room. Here the light seemed always to wax and palpitate with solemn intensity. Beneath this core of light stood a simple marble table, decked with a white cloth, gold and silver bowls, and other objects.

It was not, however, the inscrutable light beating above the altar which betrayed the brave young pharaoh into a low gasp.

Beyond the altar, a dais bore a marble plinth. On the plinth rose a figure of pure gold, with the whitest of the light pulsing upon it. It was the same symbol worked on the sunburst pendant worn by the young priestess who had passed earlier through the portico. A tall, squared column, like a beam, stood on end, crossed two-thirds of its way up by a shorter, similar beam. Reflecting the light of the white source above the altar, it glowed additionally with its own golden light, waxing so that at its strongest Amon-Ta could scarcely distinguish between the cross and its effulgence. A wide mist of shining gold beat across the room, brighter, brighter, until one's being could not withstand the brightness any longer. At that moment of entrancement, or swoon, the light sank back within the cross. The high golden figure, bathed once more in the white light, shone, regnant, in the dark chamber.

Ikhn-Om and Berynius at once frowned at Amon-Ta, Berynius again enjoining silence. The high priest indicated a seat of marble. Amon-Ta sat, gripping the edges of the bench, white-knuckled.

Ikhn-Om whispered to Berynius. Amon-Ta saw the young priest blanch, then bow his head quickly. He moved to a recess on the far side of the chamber, taking from it a black, oblong box. This he placed on a table near the altar. He dropped to his knees, his eyes closed, his face white.

Ikhn-Om moved around the altar, the cross and light behind him, so that he faced Amon-Ta. The pharaoh stared at him. He might have been anything from forty to eighty. His cheekbones were high beneath his unlined brown skin, his nose prominent. His hands were fine, with pointed fingers and strong wrists. He held them clasped before him. His long black hair was dressed with many beads, gold, silver, turquoise, ivory. His eyes were like black stars which seemed to strip one down to one's soul.

Ikhn-Om spoke: "I come here, not to save you, Amon-Ta, but in saving you to save the Temple of Faith. This temple has risen to its highest grandeur during my service, and it must be preserved as a beacon to future generations. Through countless centuries our priests have discovered the forms and means through which the Divine power may be directed. We of this temple alone know these secrets. To save our temple, I now use them in your behalf."

Berynius saw, or thought he saw, the great discs of gold hanging from the ceiling sway a little. The unease with which he had entered the chamber had grown into an ominous foreboding. He looked again at Ikhn-Om, praying that God's will be done.

Ikhn-Om moved slowly to the side table and opened the black box which Berynius had placed there. He removed two bundles wrapped in the finest of white linen, which he brought over to the altar. Setting the bundles down, he raised his arms before the cross, closing his eyes. Amon-Ta and Berynius saw a great silvery cloud envelop the high priest.

Berynius felt a slight shaking, so slight that in another moment he could not be sure it had happened. It had been as if the room had trembled.

Ikhn-Om opened his eyes and gently unwrapped the linen bundles. In the first were two faceted crystals, each the size of a man's fist, of great beauty of color. They were faceted to detail far beyond the most painstaking jeweler's effort, each having one thousand thousand sides. Each facet winked and sparkled in the glowing lights of the chamber as the crystals lay blindingly on the altar. Ikhn-Om delicately unwrapped the other bundle.

Within rested an object of crystal. Berynius averted his eyes, as if in reverence and fear, but the pharaoh gaped. He saw a skull, a life-size skull of the most natural and minute detail. In its recessed eye sockets, polished to a clear dark grey, motionless figures, or symbols, seemed encased in the fiber of the crystal itself.

Ikhn-Om lifted the skull from its linen and set it in a gold-limned circle drawn in the center of the altar. He lifted his eyes again. "Menelek is an adept hedged about with power, and ordinary means will not reach to draw his spirit from his flesh. Your sister, Srateeta, will not be difficult, but Menelek requires unanswerable power. From this skull issues power such as may not be called forth once in a thousand centuries."

Berynius heard a rumbling, as if from the corners of the room, fade away as Ikhn-Om ceased to speak. The others seemed not to have noticed, but dread filled Berynius' heart.

Ikhn-Om knelt before the three crystals, placed symmetrically on the altar. He turned the full force of his hypnotic gaze upon the white light which glowed in the air above the altar. It seemed to the pharaoh that the high priest drank in the white light through his eyes, filling

111

himself with its distillation of power. In return he poured forth a silver current, from his entire body but especially from his head, back into the white light. This exchange continued for many minutes.

Berynius felt a darkness advancing, suffocatingly, from the corners and ceiling of the room, toward its three occupants. Doom lay upon his soul as heavily as an impending thunder storm upon a summer night.

Abruptly Ikhn-Om rose, taking in each hand one of the rounded crystals. He stared into them as he held them close together. He lifted them to his forehead, and intoned with terrifying softness a terrifying blasphemy which struck Berynius' heart as a knife: "Mine the power of the Unknowable God." Then he added: "I command that Menelek's soul shall abandon his body forever, to preserve this temple."

He extended his arms, lifting the crystals into the heart of the mysterious white light, directly over the crystal skull, in its golden circle upon the marble altar.

A ray of light, dense, shining brighter than a sword blade in the sun, broke from the light-gorged crystals in the high priest's hands, down into the crystal skull. A weird gleam lit the skull from within. But it was not the resplendent pure glow Ikhn-Om had expected. Instead, an evil, murky greyish-purple illuminated the strange symbols behind the eye sockets. A dreadful sound, an obscene hum, as of lascivious death, grew to throb in the air.

Even as Ikhn-Om staggered back, aghast, the lurid light exploded from the skull, filling the Altar Room as if with poison. The floor and the walls began to shake. Amon-Ta was shouting, screaming, wild-eyed, struggling in vain to break open the silver door. Berynius, overcome by his sense of sin, prostrated himself on the floor, praying for forgiveness.

A creaking sound rang out, then the slow noise of crumbling stone. Ikhn-Om looked up to see first one, then the other of the monstrously heavy gold discs come crashing down, the first one striking Amon-Ta. The pharaoh was killed instantly. Great jagged chunks of stone fell from the ceiling, knocking statues from their pillars, smashing ornaments, burying the floor of the chamber. Berynius looked up, trying to see Ikhn-Om, as if pleading for his remorse. Then a pile of debris rushed down upon him, leaving only a thick cloud of dust.

The Altar Room was in ruins. Only the gold cross and the altar with its white light above, and Ikhn-Om who stood between them, had escaped destruction.

A voice, seeming to come from within the white light, suddenly called out: "Enough!"

The evil throbbing hum was silenced. The foul light of the skull was extinguished. The air cleared. The crystals still clenched in Ikhn-Om's hands were only jewels, with no more than jewel light.

Ikhn-Om sank to his knees in his island of safety. He looked around at the desecrated room. He thought of the two young men he had brought here, to their deaths. The fate he had just brought upon himself seized him in a hideous vision, overwhelming him with guilt. Too late conscious of the truth Lido-la had spoken, in self-loathing he cried out, striking his head against the stone floor.

"Yes," said that soft voice, permeated with unimaginable authority, which issued from the white light. "You may well regret what you have wrought, you who had risen so high in My grace. How could you have so forgotten your duty, Ikhn-Om, he of My blue star, named Servant of the Unknowable? You chose instead to use My power to be master of kings and men. Your shame is greater than Menelek's, for you have known Me, and still the pomp and intrigues of the world have seduced you from My service.

"You have brought death to innocents. You have banished Lido-la from My temple, she who alone of all of you was fit to enter it. And you have claimed to act in My name, for the sake of My temple. How may it be

113

proven to you, foolish man, that My temple is not built of stones, but of souls? Must I destroy this monument to your own vanity as proof? It is done, Ikhn-Om."

For long moments there was silence. Then, from far without, Ikhn-Om heard a faint whistling. As it rose steadily in volume and pitch, he hid his face in his hands. The desert wind had been summoned, to whip the sands higher and higher, until the Temple of Faith had been inundated, obliterated from the sight and memory of men.

"So much for your temple," the soft voice said. "Mine remains open to you. You have only to find your way to it—again."

Ikhn-Om lay broken at the foot of the golden cross. After a time he opened his eyes. In wonder, and yet in his deepest soul without surprise, he saw that the cross's golden light had extended itself, effortlessly, gently, to envelop him in its forgiveness. Tears glittered on his cheeks, like dew upon the green fields along the Nile. When he dared to look at the white light, it glowed brighter upon him.

"Yes, Ikhn-Om. Your atonement is already decided. The day will come when you will face Menelek again, and you will defeat him, the wicked priest who seeks My power but spurns My love. But not as you have tried to do, so grievously, this day. Instead you will sacrifice your will in My service.

"You will be persecuted for My sake. All will see My shadow upon you for the duration of your days, and you shall avail nothing against the danger brought upon you thereby. Only a righteous man will save you from the priests who have forgotten My way, even as you have done. And you will serve this righteous man as the voice of My power, even as your submission to My will must enable him to break the priests. You shall serve a king, even as you serve Me. And your reward, as well as his, will be My peace, and My love, at last, and everlasting."

Ikhn-Om understood these words. In another life he would be granted the chance to redeem himself, to cancel his sin. He wept in gratitude, overcome by the love and forgiveness of his master.

He continued to lie there, at the foot of the golden cross. The howling wind, muffled by the thick walls, swept the limitless sands of the desert higher upon the great edifice, the Temple of Faith. The splendor that earth had wrought was returning, as all things must, again to the oblivion of earth.

Yet the white light and the cross of gold continued to glow amid the devastation, as if that earthly death did not matter at all.

Miles to the south, Lido-la stood in the desert, accompanied by the huddle of attendants she had brought from the temple after Ikhn-Om had gone into the Altar Room with Amon-Ta and Berynius. They watched in awe and fear the wrathful cloud of sand swirling on the horizon, its magnitude terrifying, its finality implacable.

"It is a judgement," one of them whispered.

"It is merely what must be," Lido-la declared gently. "I have just communicated by spirit with Ikhn-Om. He knows his error, and he is comforted. And in our new land we will inscribe the location of the buried Temple of Faith with its things of power, for the time will come when God will have men to use them again, and rebuild anew His temple."

She smiled at them, like a mother, and her faith resurrected their own.

"Have a drink," the stranger suggested from the rim of the white stone. He filled the cup and set it on the ground between the boys. "It will help you."

Enda drank, then passed the cup to Niall. He knew what the god meant. The spring water restored him fully to the pasture, to Niall, to himself.

115

Niall drank impatiently, eying Enda over the cup. He remembered from the aftermath of Connacht what Enda must be feeling. "Well, how do you feel?" he asked, still himself awonder at the panoply and violence he had witnessed. But Enda had not merely seen it, he had relived it.

"Diarmuid," was Enda's unexpected first word. He looked at Niall. "Berynius was my little brother Diarmuid," he explained. "I'll have to take better care of him this time around." Tears came to his eyes, but he smiled.

"So you believe it all," Niall said in a low voice. He hardly knew why, but he felt almost disappointed.

Enda laughed quietly. "I believe in the sun overhead. I believe in the white stone, and in those sheep. Yes, I believe it all, just as you do. Who am I, not to believe the truth?"

Niall thought back to the bitterness and despair of the shepherd of the morning. How different he was now, calm, thoughtful, patient. His own reaction still puzzling him, he said irritably: "So, now you're satisfied with the way things are? All of a sudden you're not angry any more?"

"I'm not happy that it's necessary," Enda answered, "but I can see beyond all doubt that it is necessary." Although he had vividly identified with every negative emotion Ikhn-Om had felt on that dire day—hubris, ambition, fear—he had also shared Ikhn-Om's sense of unutterable peace, at the eager forgiveness shed upon him by the golden cross and the white light. How clearly these were with him, truer than the tree he leaned against or the staff by his side.

Suffused with serenity, Enda smiled at his friend. "I believe all will be well, somehow. And I believe that what I endure will teach me what I need to learn: that power is not our tool. We are the tools of power. We must always remember that even when we rule, we serve."

"Serve what?" Niall muttered.

116

"God," Enda whispered.

Before Niall's eyes, the Enda he had first known was restored to him, his vision filled with invisible realities, the natural acceptance of mysteries which were as clear to him as day. Power seemed to fit him like a cloak of light.

As he stared at Enda, pain slashed Niall's heart. Even the wretched comfort of their union in defiance of fate was taken from him now. He had never felt so bereft, as without warning a dizziness of grief seized him. The cruelest of agonies, absolute loneliness, seemed to laugh shrilly in his ears. Niall, who had obstinately refused to give up, the warm-hearted friend who had refused to let Enda give up—he had not seen until now that Enda was all that stood between him and defeat. Except death.

Only death could release him from the duty of kingship. But he would not submit his will to anyone—not to the councilors, not to his father, not to all his people, not to this stranger by the white stone. Not even to his beloved Enda, who had betrayed him, abandoning him to fight alone against earth and heaven to be his own master.

Niall rounded on the unflappable visitor by the white stone. "I won't give in," he said, his voice low, vehement, that of a man driven to the extremity of resistance. "Maybe Enda now sees a reason for suffering which he couldn't see before. And for his sake, I'm glad. And, yes, you showed me that I was hurting myself as well as Meta by the way I treated her. But there it stops. There's nothing, there can't be anything that will stop me from hating this prison that's my life. I'll never give in to it, to the irony that I seem to have everything, as I sit on the throne, and actually have nothing!"

The wild rage of despair blackened his vision. He found himself in Enda's arms, the shepherd having leapt to catch the prince as he wavered on his feet. "Never,"

Niall murmured bitterly, as Enda lowered him gently to the ground.

The god looked at the two boys with impersonal disinterest.

"Oh, no?" he said.

PART FOUR

The two youths found themselves, with the god, in a dusty thoroughfare irregularly bounded by the pitched tents of an army camp.

"Germany, more than three hundred fifty years ago," the god explained briefly. "This is a Roman encampment, readying for battle, if necessary, against the tribes holding this territory."

Forgetting themselves, the boys looked around eagerly, drinking in the crude vitality, the pungent life of the widespread camp. Legionaries sprawled in disorder, eating, drinking, mending armor. Over the noise of the soldiers one could hear the clanging of a hurried blacksmithing job—probably the shoeing of horses for the cavalry. Dungheaps burned, meat roasted, horses and men sweated in the sun.

"Here you will both learn the real purpose of your present life," the god continued. "That is, if anything can teach you two." Brought back to themselves, Enda and Niall glanced at each other and then at the god; but his remote expression made it evident that he intended to communicate nothing more.

Enda was reduced to uncertainty again, no longer quite the impervious prophet he had emerged as in the pasture after his experience in ancient Egypt. Here he was, apparently with something more to see. All the implications were that he and Niall had shared a past which had contributed to the necessity of their being bound together now as prince and prophet. What could have happened here in this strange land to forge the chain of destiny against which both had been straining, breathless and exhausted now, for years?

For some reason, unknown to him, he was afraid to see. He looked at Niall. The dark, handsome face was set, stiff, unwilling to know until forced. Enda silently acknowledged in his heart that this must be. Whatever it was they were to witness, they themselves had made it impossible to avoid.

A stir far down the main path of the camp rustled closer, as legionaries leapt to their feet at the approach of a broad, fit man clad in leather armor sewn with phallerae and wearing embossed gold wristguards. Frowning absently, he appeared not to notice his troops coming to attention. As he swept down the path Niall felt again that profound sense of union, the inescapable fact of identity with a figure from the past. He knew he was this man, and he knew he must follow him. Enda moved with him, and the god of the white stone as well, silent and all-observant.

The man's progress down the dusty way was stopped by a young page, who blinked nervously as he accosted his quarry. "General Quintus," he began, "the Captain Honorius bid me tell you that a message has arrived and awaits you in your tent."

"Yes, yes, lad," Quintus said impatiently, "am I not on my way there now?" He brushed by the boy, quickening his pace. Grey threads in his cropped, curly black hair glinted in the sun as he strode on, his dark eyes seeing beyond the lively squalor of the camp, and not liking what they saw.

Abruptly, he turned in at a large tent set a little apart. A camp bed stood low in one corner, a silver ewer and basin rested on a wooden stand nearby, and two chairs were placed on one side of the map tray, with a wine-table between them. From one of these chairs jumped up a young man, tall, with curly black hair and black eyes.

"Honorius," Quintus said.

"Father," the young man answered. "Here is the message from Caesar."

Quintus took the scroll, broke the seal, and rapidly scanned its contents. Honorius, watching anxiously, saw pain graven deeply on his father's brow. There was no need to ask what the scroll contained.

Quintus raised his eyes from the scroll to his son and said heavily: "Yes, it's what I feared. Only the gods know how Caesar feels justified in breaking a treaty I was empowered to make. There is nothing I can say to Wulfa to avert catastrophe."

"Wulfa is a proud man," Honorius said carefully.

"And so am I," Quintus flashed. "Read this! Caesar has the insolence to hint that I was influenced by my friendship with Wulfa to bargain away the best interests of Rome! It is tantamount to a charge of treason! Caesar forgets himself. He may be commander-in-chief, but our line is as exalted as his. The Terentii served Rome before the Caesars emerged from the mud to claim descent from Venus!"

Honorius' jaw set as he read the scroll. Caesar had made no accusations, but his silky language drew delicate inferences of collusion from the fact of his father's longstanding friendship with Wulfa, chieftain and warleader of the Germanic tribes which held this valuable province now at issue. Quintus, in command at the frontier, had treated with Wulfa for a suitable division of the territory, part for Rome, part retained by Wulfa's compatriots. But now Caesar had gainsaid Quintus' proposals. That Quintus had acted throughout with strict integrity, proposing a peaceful resolution so as to avoid worthless bloodshed, was a fact that Caesar seemed to discount. Caesar demanded all the territory, and Quintus was herewith ordered to execute this order, by any means neces-sary.

"He has insulted our house," Honorius said, looking up at his father.

"We will deal with that in due time," Quintus replied. "Now we have more urgent problems." He turned to pace the enclosure, hard discipline allowing him no other out-let for his anguish. "I have known Wulfa for twenty years," he burst out. "Since we first skirmished in Gaul, and then were both of the treating party. He may be a barbarian, but he is a good man. I have no closer friend on earth. And he is a man of absolute honor. He will never understand that I must obey an order of my commander. He will consider me forsworn, a liar, a dishonored wretch."

"But you are not," Honorius answered quickly. "If Wulfa cannot understand that your honor rests upon obey-ing your commander, it is unfortunate. But you are not to blame."

"Wulfa will not see it that way," Quintus said sadly. "In his code a man must first and foremost be true to what he knows is right. He must not submit his will to another's."

"Wulfa is not a Roman," Honorius said simply.

Quintus stood for several minutes, staring blindly into the sand of the map tray. A tension emanated from him such as one senses from those who foresee the loss of something indispensably dear—an agony of waiting which yet wishes to stay the blow. Then his head snapped up and he barked at Honorius: "What are we waiting for? Order the troops to arm and dispose themselves. After I have spoken to Wulfa battle is inevitable."

Honorius looked at his father's averted face and went without a word. Quintus raised his fist and smashed it down on the map tray. "If it were not for the honor of Rome," he muttered, "I would sacrifice my own to keep my word, even though it would disgrace my son and line forever. But I cannot. A Roman is not his own man. He is Rome's."

Within a half-hour a messenger had been dispatched to Wulfa's camp, begging a conference between the two leaders. The Romans were prepared to march, readying themselves with that amazing quickness which was already being called Caesar-speed. Quintus held no illusions as to Wulfa's provision for battle. He would come to meet Quintus at the center of the field—with his whole army at his back. When either man raised his right arm, battle would begin.

Quintus waited only for the return of the messenger before mounting his big chestnut war stallion. A troop accompanied him, the rest of the legion hanging some distance back. Upon nearing the copse of trees agreed on as the meeting-place, Quintus signaled to the troop to halt. He rode forward with only Honorius and another officer, Marcellus, on either side.

The magnificent horses, restive and arrogant, stamped and shied, but the three men controlled them without apparent effort. The sun shone on the broad field, bounded to the north by the broad, deep river with steep banks, and to the south and east by thinly wooded hills. To the west waited the Roman legion, the shields and shortswords of the footsoldiers stabbing the eye with myriad points of light. Already the carrion birds circled overhead, awaiting the clash of metal and the scent of fresh blood.

Honorius avoided looking at his father's face; not for fear of what he might see, but because it would be invasive to search a man's countenance. But he knew without asking of the pain behind his father's impassive mask, of the dilemma of seeming dishonored either to his countrymen or his old friend, no matter what course he took. Honorius had no fear that his father would retreat from his duty as a Roman. He wished for Quintus' sake that Wulfa would understand.

A muffled noise from the east suddenly broke louder over the hill as three horsemen appeared, backed by a disorderly but impressive mounted troop perhaps two hundred strong. As these advanced, the main host of Wulfa's army came over the hill at some distance behind, spreading themselves over the plain. Their numbers were such that a considerable portion must fan across the lower range of the hillside.

The troop halted while the three horsemen cantered forward to where the Romans waited by the copse of ash trees. Quintus waited without moving, his face impassive, his dark eyes gazing steadily at the approaching chieftain and war leader.

Enda and Niall, accompanied by the silent god, recognized the great, blond German as he rode up and reined in his horse so decisively that the animal neither jibbed nor drooped, but stood at watchful attention. Neither his fierceness, nor his size, nor the long, blond mustaches sweeping across his chest could conceal from either youth this man's identification with Enda. The quiet shepherd, ignorant of the most basic arts of war but for what Niall had shown him, and what his soul remembered, perhaps from this very time, had once been a warrior from the cold north—and the friend, and now it seemed the enemy too, of the Roman lord who lived now as the prince of Meath.

Knowing Enda as Wulfa completed Niall's submersion into union with Quintus. He felt the Roman general's agony and frustration as fully as he had ever felt frustration and rage at his present conflict of duty and will. Enda, due to his own nature and his illumination at reliving his past as Ikhn-Om, was fortunately able to remain more emotionally detached from the gripping clash of different codes occurring before his eyes. Nevertheless he could feel, as one with him, Wulfa's anger, his scorn and sense of betrayal which left him implacable, incapable of condition or compromise.

124

Pride and enmity burned with the heat of outraged affection in Wulfa's ice-blue eyes. He sat his big horse in silence, waiting for Quintus to speak. He spared not a glance for Honorius, whom he had always loved. He stared, unblinking, at his old friend. Quintus closed his eyes for several seconds, then opened them into that haughty glare of blue, bright and hurtful as the noon sun to a man long concealed in darkness.

"Wulfa," Quintus began. "As I informed you by messenger three weeks ago, it came to my ears that my commander, Gaius Julius Caesar, was not pleased with my treaty regarding this territory which you and I found mutually satisfactory. Since I understood that I had full powers to treat as I saw fit, I sent to Caesar for clarification of his wishes in this matter, pointing out the benefits of a peaceful resolution. I also sent to you, explaining the situation and begging your indulgence as to the delay in concluding our treaty." Quintus paused. "Your response caused me great uneasiness."

Wulfa never moved. His lips were as hard as carved stone. Honorius watched his father tensely, but Quintus did not falter.

"Despite the tone of your answer, you were good enough to wait for Caesar's reply to my message. That message, as you know, arrived today. I have hoped, and prayed, these three weeks, for the only answer either of us could wish. Unfortunately, I hoped and prayed in vain. Caesar commands me to claim this entire territory for Rome by whatever means necessary." Here Quintus did fall silent, as if acknowledging that further speech from him would be useless until Wulfa had made retreat from doom impossible for both with one word.

Looking at Wulfa, Honorius saw for the first time that standards foreign to oneself could engender a principled and noble rage in an opponent, justifying his opposition. This may be one of the most important realizations a soul can ever make. It is wiser to be certain that one is right than to be certain another is wrong.

Quintus had spoken haltingly in Wulfa's Germanic dialect. When Wulfa at last answered, he used a heavily-accented but fluent Latin. Yet Enda and Niall understood everything, as they had done earlier, and in the far mist-hung past of Ikhn-Om and the Temple of Faith.

"You are forsworn," Wulfa said coldly. "Your word is worthless, your honor a phantom exorcised by expediency. The faith we held as friends is rendered a lie. It was thus from the moment you informed me that your oath could be, might be, rescinded by another's will. From that moment we have owed each other nothing." Then his eyes returned to Quintus, never wavering, made fearless through anger to face this death.

Fury seethed through Quintus as well. Not fury against Rome, nor even Caesar, but rage at his own powerlessness to alter this situation except for the worse. What Rome demanded, he must give. What friendship with Wulfa demanded, he must deny. When a man must choose between his duty and his desire, was it not the greater part to sacrifice love for honor? Was not duty above all things sacred? Yet he could not resign himself to this end.

"The error was mine," he said in a hard voice. "I mistook my authority. This result is regrettable to us both, but it is unavoidable." Honorius thought, as he looked from one leader to the other, of Caesar's implication that Quintus had been ready to barter away Rome's interest to avoid war with his old friend; but he knew his father would never plead for Wulfa's pardon with that charge. Nor, sighed Honorius inwardly, would it soften Wulfa in any case.

"Your treachery is preferable to your hypocrisy," Wulfa said with deep disgust. "It is now clear that the friendship of the last twenty years has been cultivated with some aim like this in mind. I was a fool to believe that a Roman could understand the sacredness of friendship.

Among my people a man's word is his most binding guarantee, especially when given between friends. Nothing, not even the gods, could cause us to cheat where our honor is pledged, because it is the gods whom we obey when we love one another in trust. You have done more than break your word, you have profaned the holiness of a people who welcomed you as one of foreign birth but noble spirit. I am responsible for permitting this insult to my people and my gods. Therefore I must wash away this dishonor with blood."

Quintus had paled with each condemnatory sentence, till Honorius and Marcellus saw him bloodless, even his lips as livid as a winter sky. Perhaps it was only now that he realized how much he had lost; perhaps it had been Wulfa's vengeance to make clear the extent of this loss. He whispered: "If I had no master...."

Then he was silent.

"My only master is here," Wulfa replied scornfully, touching his heart. "For it is here that the gods speak to me. And they have told me what I must do."

He took his right fist from his heart and raised it high in the air. His axehead shone in the silent, swimming light.

Without further words each triad of horsemen turned and galloped back to take their places leading the armies. As soon as Quintus was beneath the banner of Rome the legion charged, trumpets shouting, horses screaming, hundreds of hooves, thousands of feet churning the ground. Coming toward them, with hoarse cries meant to terrify, axes and spears tied with horsehair plumes swinging and stabbing, swarmed the German army. The two hosts met with a force that seemed to shake the land. Cries and the stench of new-spilled blood rose to where the ravens circled above the fight, in lazy swoops of obscene ease.

The fight took several directions, the first to show any advantage for either side occurring to the north, where part of a wing of the German force had been cut off and backed against the river by a remorseless Roman thrust. They retreated desperately into the shallows, but the river bed dropped off steeply and the currents clutched at and submerged them. Legionaries stood on the bank, waiting to cut down any who struggled out of the current and onto the shingle. With no avenue of escape, hundreds died. Behind the legionaries on the bank a living wall of massed Roman ranks protected them from the valiant efforts of other Germans to rescue the drowning men in the river which now ran red.

To the southwest Quintus fought doggedly. The Germans, it seemed, prized the glory of killing the enemy commander, so at any given moment Quintus contended with three attackers. The numbers coming against him were such that he was forced into defensive action only, often killing but necessarily relying on the picked guard surrounding him to thin out the swell of eager mounted spearmen or ambitious footsoldiers.

The pain and rage within him had dulled, as the skill that was second nature took over to make of him an efficient fighting machine. His only concession to human feeling, aside from a perhaps subconscious avoidance of Wulfa, was to keep an eye out for Honorius.

However, that young officer needed no protection. Both his swordsmanship and horsemanship were brilliant. He seemed to hear the singing directions of his sword, and feel the brave spirit of his mount, as if the rigors of battle had elevated his senses to an exquisite consciousness, where perception had grown to instant intuition. With all his burdens and the press of the moment, Quintus was able to see Honorius cut cleanly through the onslaught of tow-colored giants, with seeming invincibility, and cherish a glow of pride. Quintus still had the honor of his line to fight for, and Rome.

Wulfa led repeated, savage attempts to rescue his men caught at the river, actually buckling, then breaking the Roman phalanx, cutting down scores of legionaries with amazing strength and speed. He cleared a broad path for those Germans still alive on the shingle to pour onto the disordered Romans, screaming in triumph, swinging their axes like scythes through a hay field. They yelled Wulfa's name, exhorting themselves to greater effort by calling upon the man through whom the gods led their fights on earth.

Two hours slogged by, deep now in slimy mud, then three, and beyond. The sun was ripe and orange now, falling to the distant edge of the western plain. Ravens, wings flapping loosely, had already settled on slain soldiers, left as the fighting moved east and north. The Roman camp hospital had been set up near a small wood to the west, and orderlies already carried wounded legionaries back to the doctors.

For the tide seemed to have turned against the Germans, despite Wulfa's heroic rescue at the river, and his general inspiration of his army throughout the battle. The Romans had managed to gain the other boundaries of the field, and now pressed on the Germans, to drive them with a ring of shortswords into the center of the field, or into the river, as the lie of the land beckoned. The Germans fought like men possessed, with the excess of bravery which is the other face of hopelessness, but their state was such that, if events did not soon reverse the battle's course, the best they could hope for would be the chance to break and run.

It may be that Wulfa sensed this growing danger of accepted defeat, and chose to eviscerate it by a symbolic gesture. Or perhaps he, like Quintus, had avoided their meeting, and blamed the threatening vanquishment of the Germans on what he saw as cowardice. Would the gods crown with victory a man who hesitated to avenge their insult?

From whatever cause, Wulfa suddenly gave a great cry, heard at the farthest reaches of the field, and galloped toward the band of fighting still thick around the Roman general. To everyone, German and Roman, he seemed borne forward through the tangle of skirmishings as the sun in its flight is borne through bodiless clouds. His bright blue eyes gleamed with the power of a commitment which cannot now be broken.

A shout went up from Quintus' guard. Warned, Quintus swung his back away from Wulfa, as several Romans spurred themselves between Quintus' other flank and the Germans he had been holding at bay.

There was a clash as axe met Roman sword that jarred the bones of all who heard it. It was like a signal to those fighting on distant parts of the field, for most men, German and Roman, held their blows as they saw the two generals engaged.

Almost before the blow, Quintus' stallion recoiled, then leaped forward, lashing out with forefeet at Wulfa's black stallion. The black stallion, hit hard, wheezed, bending down his forebody, trying to catch his breath. In this vulnerable moment Wulfa leaned forward on his horse's neck to swing a cruel sideswipe with his axe at Quintus' forearm, which the Roman held not raised, but with strong twisted wrist, ready for an opening in Wulfa's guard. The German axe whistled by harmlessly, its deadly track a bright arc of air where Quintus had been a second before. Wulfa's mount, recovering, retreated a couple of paces, then plunged forward again at Wulfa's spur. Quintus reined his chestnut sharply and met Wulfa's advance, parried once more the fall of the axe, then wheeled, thrust, was met, and quickly thrust again, this time slashing Wulfa's left arm. Wulfa, blood from the flesh wound running red over his gold armband, seemed not to notice the cut of the steel blade. The axe, black with dried blood, swung again, and was met again by the gleaming, slender sword of Quintus.

Wulfa did battle savagely, with strength almost incredible, and speed not often found together with such power. Quintus fought coolly, eyes everywhere at once. This cool vision took in Honorius, who more than held his own against Wulfa's followers. He never moved more than a few paces from his father, defending his left with untiring diligence.

For ten minutes which seemed to all those watchers on the field like ten hours, the two generals fought an even match. Quintus now had a grazed calf where Wulfa's axe had touched him, but he bore no other mark. Nor had Quintus slipped through Wulfa's guard again. The two superb beasts the generals sat fought like third arms for their masters, swerving, kicking, even biting at each other. Honorius, aided by a few other officers, fought off the Germans who had crowded around Wulfa. Yet, even with the field clear to meet each other, Quintus and Wulfa seemed stalemated, warriors of equal skill waiting for the stroke of luck which would give the verdict of the clashing gods.

Perhaps a quick eye and hand to match are all that luck can be. Honorius, pressing an advantage, lunged forward, pursuing the German he had just wounded. At the same moment Wulfa's stallion put a foot false, pitching him away from Quintus as the horse stumbled almost to its knees. Quintus pulled his stallion back a pace or two, with martial courtesy, to allow Wulfa to recover. Wulfa, however, between Quintus and Honorius, saw in a moment that his follower was too weakened to escape Honorius' attack. Even before his mount had regained its footing, with no time or need for thought Wulfa drove his axe deep into Honorius' side, exposed as he lifted his sword for the final, lethal cut. The axehead thudded and grated on bone. Honorius sat his horse for the most fragile shadow of a second, as if in the first shock he could not summon the strength to fall. Then he wavered and slumped to the churned, slimy ground, his fall quickened by the bolting of his frantic stallion, screaming as the blood gushed over its mane.

Both older men watched him fall; then, as if responding to a call, each swung to face the other. Wulfa's face was stern, but not cruel. Quintus spurred his chestnut onto

Wulfa, slashing down on his neck. He brutally yanked his sword from the wound even before the half-severed head lolled sickeningly on Wulfa's shoulder. Wulfa's eyes protruded, his tongue swelled as he choked on his blood; then he fell underneath his wild horse, writhed convulsively, and lay still.

Quintus leapt from his saddle, kneeling in the muck to slip his arm gently behind his son's neck, turning his face near. The blood that bubbled on Honorius' lips was dark red, heart's-blood. His lung had been opened by the axe.

Unbelievably, to Quintus, Honorius tried to smile, though he could make only the slightest movement of his lips. His black eyes turned up white, but he had seen his father's grief. On one last great shuddering breath he whispered: "Duty, duty, duty." Then life left him.

The famous Roman litany burned into Quintus' brain like poison poured upon a wound. Bitterness strangled him as he looked from his dead son—the end of his ancient line—to Wulfa's mangled body, the long yellow hair stiff with drying blood, the great arms flung wide in the agony of death. He had done what duty required of him. He had obeyed that dishonored jackal named Caesar, and in return he had lost his beloved son, seen his line end forever on a battlefield which, no matter what Rome would believe, had been unworthy to extinguish a proud Roman name. And he had broken faith with Wulfa. He had betrayed his friend's trust and spilt his blood. And he could not endure to live, to hear the praise of Rome ring in his ears for this day's work.

Quintus did not loose his son's body. With his right hand he took Honorius' dagger from its sheath. "I renounce Rome," he said. "I renounce my rank and my service," he said, as his voice rose, drenched with anguish, so that his men turned to him, stunned. "I renounce duty!" he cried. "I will be free! And if death is the only door to freedom, then willingly I pass through it!" He tore off his dented and spattered breastplate and hilted his son's dagger in his heart.

Horrified, several of his officers rushed to him, but they were too late. Quintus had fallen across his son's body. Oddly enough, his empty right hand lay extended, as if in appeal, or reconciliation, toward Wulfa.

Time had worn away back in the pasture of the white stone. The sun was halfway down the sky toward the west, but the boys scarcely noticed. They found themselves sitting under the oak, shaken by what they had witnessed, yet with a sense of release from bonds of which they had only become aware on loosing them. The silent god rested upon the rim of the white stone, watching the prince and the shepherd.

All at once Niall seemed to find it easy to eat his words. For years he had fought with bitter resentment against his fate, but now that resistance had vanished, like mist at sunrise.

"Everything makes perfect sense now. Everything— why I am who I am. Why you're who you are. Quintus was wrong, and—Honorius was right. No one is free of duty. Everyone must follow the path laid before him. That's why I'm the prince now, to learn that Quintus was wrong. The more power you have, the less right you have to your own will."

Already there was a new maturity in Niall's face, the dark eyes calmer, the fine lips set in a strong but easy line. He grinned at his friend, releasing in one bound the joy of youth he had kept rigidly capped for so long. "You're quite a warrior. No wonder you were so good at swordplay when we were young."

Enda, who was not trained to war as Niall was, took a little longer to be at peace with what he had been and done in another life. "Quintus had to do what he did," he said slowly, thinking aloud his way to understanding. "But Wulfa was right, too. I can feel that he was right. He had no choice but to avenge the betrayal of his people and his gods. He felt he had brought that betrayal on his people because his friendship with Quintus had led him to trust where he would not have trusted another Roman, a stranger."

He brooded for a moment, then concluded: "Quintus was right, and Wulfa was right. I don't know how it could have happened any other way."

"It couldn't have," Niall said briskly. "Don't worry about it. We're still friends, aren't we?"

Enda laughed, his sunny nature restored, the looming shadows of his isolation and uncertain future fled like phantoms in the light of his reborn faith. "Still friends," he said, "though I'm not sure why. I can think of easier tasks than prophesying for a pig-headed prince. You're going to have to learn to listen to me."

"I'll listen to the gods when they speak," Niall retorted. "You I wouldn't even trust to find a horse in a stable."

The two boys bantered for a while, lying in the shade of the oak. It was Niall who noticed, in a careless glance toward the white stone, that the god of the spring and the stone had gone. This roused them for a minute or two, but they were tired, more worn out from their violent emotions than from any cause of time or body, and they lay back on the green turf once more, looking at the sky through the waving boughs overhead, too lazy even to melt clouds.

"One thing," said Enda suddenly, after a few minutes of contented silence between them. "I know it's silly to feel this way now, when we're who we are, Niall and Enda—but I'm sorry about Honorius." He turned his head as he lay to look at Niall.

He thought Niall had a strange expression on his face as he said, "Yes, Honorius." Even his voice sounded altered. "That must have happened as it should, too."

They fell silent again. Enda's eyes closed. In a little time he thought he heard a voice. It was the god's voice, saying: "You have cleared the pasture, and the spring with its white stone, of your harmful will and passion. Keep them clear. I will be there with you. You will not see me but you will know. You are one who will always know."

Niall and Enda wakened at the touch of a man, who stooped between them as they lay beneath the ancient oak. A tall man, powerful and fit, with silver cords braided into his dark hair and Niall's eyes in his sun-browned face. A sword, sheathed, hung at his side. Its scabbard was gilded, and the great jewels of its hilt burned in the westering sun, red, blue, green. His clothes were fine, in four vivid colors. On the hand that touched Enda shone a great ruby, set in a gold ring designed with fluid, harmonious lines.

Niall and Enda lifted up, Enda with the suddenness of one quickly wakened, moreover by a stranger. But Niall moved more urgently. "Father?" he said, struggling to his feet.

His father looked at him for a moment. Then he lifted his hand to the troop that had ridden over the hills with him into the pasture, signaling them to withdraw. Enda, who had not even noticed the finely mounted troop in realizing that it was King Cathal, Niall's father, who stood over him, now cast an anxious eye for his sheep. He relaxed, a little, as he spied a soldier gathering his straying flock, evidently on Cathal's order.

As the troop turned and cantered away a hundred paces, Cathal looked back to Niall. "Well," he said, "and who is this with you?"

135

Enda, pale before, now flushed scarlet. He looked dumbly at Niall, pale himself. "This is Enda son of Mahon, who keeps his father's sheep in this pasture. He's a friend of mine," Niall managed to answer.

"I'd guessed that much," his father said dryly. Enda fell to his knee and bowed his head. "Well, Enda," the king said.

"My lord," Enda said, but his voice cracked feebly. He was not afraid, but the encounter was outside his normal scope. Having made his obeisance, he lifted his head and met Cathal's gaze. A shock ran through him, as if the king had plumbed the depths of his soul. In Cathal's eyes he saw more than similarity to Niall. Unmistakably he recognized the Roman officer, Honorius.

Cathal registered Enda's altered expression as the shepherd stared at him. Did Enda imagine it, or did the king's dark eyes change subtly as he gave stare for stare, conveying to the boy both confirmation and kindly forgiveness? The king smiled, and Enda felt the turf beneath his knee again.

Afterward, thinking of those few moments when his eyes locked with Cathal's, Enda wondered if Niall's father knew of the past also. It seemed unlikely. Yet, Enda thought, if the god had come to Niall and him, why could he not have come to Cathal—perhaps when Cathal was a boy, unwilling to shoulder the task he had accepted? Did the god of the stone perhaps come to many people, in many differing forms and ways, to do for them what he had done for Niall and Enda? And did these people, if the god indeed came in whatever form—even in the form of a dream—did they gradually forget his visit and his message? Or were there many who kept a secret such as Enda and Niall would keep?

"Sit down, Enda," the king said agreeably, seating himself on the rim of the white stone. "And you, Niall. So, trouble again, eh? I assume Enda's heard your side of things, for I gather this is a friendship of some duration."

"Yes," Niall said in response to both his father's surmises. "But no more trouble," he added, his voice firm, his manner responsible, and more than all, the old love for his father plain in his eyes for the king to see. "I'm over all that now. I know where my duty lies, and I want nothing more than to live up to it. I'm sorry for the worry I've caused everyone—you, the councilors..." He paused, recalling that bitter confrontation in the palace gardens, then finished bravely: "And Meta. I've already put that right, as far as I can. And I'm ready now to make everything else right as a prince of Meath."

The king maintained his calm demeanor, but there was a gleam of something in his face as he answered: "I'm very glad to hear it. Perhaps we can talk more this evening, if you can spare me the time from Meta. But now...."

"I want to say one more thing, sir," Niall interrupted. "It doesn't matter that Enda's here, he knows it already. It's just that...I know everything you've ever done for me has been to try and help me fit myself for what I must do later on. I want you to know I know, that's all. And that I'm grateful."

Nothing more could be said. "I know, boy," Cathal said, resting one hand lightly on Niall's shoulder, in his old way. "I've always known. And now we must be going. Do you realize the day is nearly over? We came looking for you before noon, and when we found you gone the court was frantic to send out search-parties. Let's get back and relieve their fears, shall we? At least there'll be no further misunderstandings. You'll come openly to visit Enda, as any honorable man visits another. But before we go, I need a drink. The wine is off in my saddlebag, but this spring looks remarkably pure."

"Here is the stone cup, my lord," Enda said, taking it from its niche in the white stone. "It is as ancient as the spring itself. They say the spring's god carved it himself, and hollowed the white stone, and that he still watches over the pasture."

The two young men's eyes met as Enda handed the cup full of sweet water to the king. "Does he indeed?" Cathal said after a long, refreshing drink. "Then surely Niall and you will be safer here, by the god's white stone, than anywhere else in the kingdom. I thank you, Enda, and perhaps I shall see you again before long—if Niall ever invites me to accompany him on a visit to your pasture. We shall have to leave now, Niall."

Enda thought it wisest to retreat on ceremony. "Goodbye, my lord king," he said, dropping to his knee again. "Goodbye, my lord prince."

"Goodbye, Enda son of Mahon," Cathal said, amused.

"Goodbye, Enda," Niall echoed, embarrassed as Enda knelt before him. Enda looked up with a mischievous gleam, laughing silently at Niall. "All right," Niall muttered as he turned to follow his father, "you'll pay for that next time I'm here."

"Find me a girl somehow and I promise I'll never kneel to you again," Enda murmured. Niall flashed him another glance, grinned, then ran, catching up with his father. The troop advanced to meet the king and the prince. Cathal and Niall mounted and set off at the head of the troop, south, toward the capital and the palace.

As they crested the hill the two lead figures turned and waved to Enda, who still knelt by the white stone and the spring under the oak. The air was cool, for the sun was orange in the west. As the steady hoofbeats of the troop faded into nothing, Enda rose to sit on the edge of the white stone. He placed the cup in its niche and sat quietly, not truly listening, but hearing nonetheless the delicate singing of the air, of the meadow, of the oak and the white stone. Some distance off his sheep, herded neatly by Cathal's soldier, cropped turf and clover placidly.

After a time, which might have been a moment or an hour, Enda felt what he had been waiting to feel. The coming was as tangible and normal as the coming of one through a door. The presence was here, by its white stone. The god, the stranger, the visitor who brought with him such riches of truth was here, and would come again. He would not speak nor make himself visible any more. But he would see and bless all that passed in the holy shade of the oak. Niall would come back, freely now, and with Enda feel the presence and hear the light singing of the pasture and the white stone. Here they would always remember; here, they could never forget.

The light slid down, after a time, over Enda, in a green-gold splendor. The sun gracefully submitted to another sinking. Enda came to himself, noticing that the presence of the white stone had gone. He saw also, in a glance at the liquid sky, that he was long since due home, and that the sheep had wandered again. He snatched up his stick and ran off to drive the sheep gently before him, home.

PART FIVE

The great hall of the king's palace of Meath glowed with waxlight in the dusk of an autumn evening. Jewels glinted, rich fabrics flashed in heavy splendor. High on the walls and from the great roof beams banners flaunted in the currents of air raised by the stoked fire, lit against the twilight chill. The mingled scents of roast meats, fowl, and fish spiced the air. Above all the tumult of light and color, the noise of a few hundred voices rose triumphantly. The court sat at table, each place designated and rigidly adhered to by rank, that most vague and inflexible rule. Slaves served the royals and nobles, then joined the lower members of the court in helping themselves. Wine and mead poured. Sweetmeats passed down the table from the king's chair, with a special pause at the traveling singer and poet, in the seat of honor reserved for these most welcome visitors.

It seemed especially fit that he had arrived today, to celebrate the king's return to court. Cathal had been obliged to take an impressive armed force to the edge of his domain, where his boundaries ran with those of a greedy, young king, who (it was reported) had authorized forays into Meath. Some looting had been the ostensible purpose, but Cathal knew that if he failed to respond decisively his neighbor would soon launch an organized attack. Accordingly, he and his force had ridden out, inspected the damage, and then boldly crossed the bound-

ary to issue a challenge. Cathal's superior force cowed
the young king; chastened, he accepted Cathal's terms,
including a sizeable indemnity. The people of Meath
would be safe from his depredations for some time to
come.

Niall had gone with his father. It had been his first
real military excursion, and except for being glad to return to Meta, he was disappointed that so little had come
of such a promising excuse for action. He knew his father
had acted wisely, but he was fifteen and quite ready for a
fight. In the months since Cathal had discovered him with
Enda in the pasture of the white stone Niall had grown
increasingly eager to test himself against the challenges
which made themselves available. His main regret was
that these opportunities had been neither as hard nor as
frequent as he would have liked.

His dark skin glowed with health in the golden
waxlight, his eyes bright, alert. The wooden plate chased
with gold before him held the remains of viands demol-
ished as if by a young wolf. Meta, beside him, smiled con-
tentedly at her husband's return. In five months their first
child would be born. Niall took her hand under the table
and squeezed it, but his eyes still roved the hall, noting
everything, assessing it for value as a strengthener of his
soul.

He had been gone for three weeks, and had not seen
Enda for a week before leaving. He intended to run up to
the pasture tomorrow, if he could steal the time. Enda
would be fascinated to hear about the campaign, quiet as
it was—all the details of camp life, the march, the awe of
the peasants on seeing the king. Enda would smile, now,
at that last.

Nothing had changed in Enda's circumstances since
that final day of encounter with the god of the white stone
and the spring, but Enda himself had. Not quite the boy
he had been when Niall first met him—manhood had
made him understand why his innocence threatened the

world most people accepted as the limit of experience—but innocent even so, for all that a self-aware innocence is of all qualities the most difficult to sustain. He had grown amazingly serene, considering what his life was. He seemed content to wait upon the moment to reveal to him the urgencies of fate as they became relevant. In him faith had become sight.

This is not to say that he no longer noticed the hostility of his father and neighbors, nor that his blood ceased to burn in his veins with desire for a woman. But this latter, at least, Niall could do something about. He had seen, over the long summer days, how Enda had grown pale, and hollow in the cheek, consumed from within by a fire which had never had the chance to sear Niall. Yet Enda never complained. His silence prevented Niall from open commiseration, or even an offer of help. He had had an idea, however, while away, and he meant now to execute it, with the help of a lively young girl, a former leman of his own. They remembered each other fondly, and he was certain she would agree to a charitable deception involving a strong young man of her own class. Meta, of course, must never know. But in the happiest of marriages there were secrets to keep, where men and women were wise.

A temporary break in the roar of talk in the hall prompted Niall to seize the chance to chat with his wife without braying. He leaned toward her, but he never spoke. A woman seated a few places below Meta had taken advantage of the lull to announce juicily:

"Has everyone heard about that shepherd who was caught by the priests in blasphemy? Well, tonight is the full moon. There'll be a sacrifice in Nemet at moonrise, you can be sure."

In the babble of excited gossip which followed, Niall felt like a man drowning in icy seas. The fullness of his horror grew from his certainty. It must be Enda. He sat, stunned, able only to let horror act upon him.

Alarmed, Meta looked at her husband's white face and tardily put two and two together. "Oh, my lord," she whispered frantically, taking Niall's unresponsive hand, "I am so sorry I did not tell you instantly! We have all heard about the blasphemer, but I never thought of your friend! They have kept him now for two weeks, and tonight—"

Meta swallowed, and as she did so Niall knew that the cold weight bearing him down was fear. With the thought came his release. The noise in the hall prevented his hearing the first informant's conversation. Leaping to his feet, knocking his heavy chair over backwards, he grabbed the heavy bell from its place before his father and rang it for silence.

Even for the prince it was a terrible breach of protocol to usurp this prerogative from the king, the more so as the visiting singer, in his poet's robe of honor, was tuning his harp to begin the evening's tale. People gaped, shocked dumb. Queen Cathla raised her eyebrows in well-bred affront, and the king stared in grave rebuke. Then as he registered his son's white face and shaking hands, he quickly said: "Niall, what is wrong?"

Unheeding, Niall turned to the noblewoman who had spoken first, saying fiercely: "Tell me everything you know about this shepherd taken in blasphemy." Then, as the startled lady hesitated, he shouted in a fury of desperation: "Talk, woman! This may be the most important deed you ever perform!"

Too frightened to look at the distraught prince, the woman addressed herself to Meta. It appeared that the druid council had received several reports within a short period of time about this peasant—his name unknown, the court knew only that he was a shepherd—claiming that he practiced magic, in flagrant defiance of the laws restricting such activities to the druids themselves. In consequence the young man had been 'summoned' to the council hall, where he was confronted with witnesses who recounted story after story of his uncanny behavior and

strange manner. Why, even his own father and sisters tes-
tified against him, adamantly disavowing any share of his
illegal goings-on...though, it was rumored, his mother had
refused to speak against him, even after her husband had
beaten her....

The evidence had been overwhelming, and the guilty
one summarily sentenced to death. But, as everyone knew,
the druids must wait until the full moon to sacrifice the
blasphemer to the goddess, so he had been held under
arrest in the grove of Nemet. One more thing, the lady
added; her own maid had happened to be in the way as
the prisoner was led from the council hall, and the girl
swore that the priests in their wisdom had acted rightly;
for even though his flesh was bruised and his clothes torn,
and his red hair smeared with dust where the angry crowd
had pelted him with clods and stones, his blue eyes held
a calmness impossible under the circumstances to one innocent of secret knowledge.

Cathal had long since grasped the situation. Without
doubt it was Niall's friend Enda who was sentenced to
die under the crooked knife. He watched as Niall's mouth
thinned to an ugly line, and his eyes flashed with scorn
more noble than any royal anger, while the voluble lady
protested that the criminal could not possibly be innocent if he had been found guilty. He saw Niall look up
blindly, and say into the puzzled, dead silence: "My horse,
and my sword. Immediately."

"No!" Not Cathal, but Meta had spoken. Aghast at her
own presumption, nonetheless she clutched at Niall's
sleeve. "If you profane Nemet—" It was not necessary to
finish. No one in that hall, nor in the kingdom, would
willingly go within a mile of Nemet on the night of the
full moon.

Without violence but without forbearance Niall withdrew his sleeve from Meta's hand. "If I do not," he said
in a low clear voice, hard as flint, "I will profane every-

145

where I walk for the rest of my life." He turned from her to find his father, risen, standing in his path.

Must he defy here, too? If he must, he would, without a second thought, except for disappointment that he had so far misread his father, and that the new intimacy with him had been only a delusion, now to end forever.

Cathal read this, and perhaps other messages as well, in his son's eyes. He said gently: "I see nothing else for you to do." He paused, then asked: "Will you accept an escort?"

"No," Niall said, gratitude shading his voice, which only those two could hear, or understand. "And there's no time anyway."

The king nodded. It was what he had expected. "Go then," he answered, pushing Niall toward the door.

On so desperate a ride Niall would normally have cursed the moon for delaying her rise, and so keeping his way dark and dangerous. Tonight the only prayer in his heart was that the moon would stay behind the hills until he had got to Nemet and thwarted her bloody goddess.

The only thought in his mind was of Wulfa and Quintus, of that dreadful battlefield where each had died of the bitterness of love betrayed. He was being offered now, as he had been denied then, the chance to risk all else, even his life, for the sake of that love. He must not betray Enda, his trust, his faith, by failing now. He must not betray himself. By the white stone itself, he must reach Nemet before the moon rose, else all he had seen and known was meaningless.

Did he imagine it, or was that a glimmer of brightness at the edge of the sky? Niall drove his heels into his horse's ribs and brought his lash down. The horse snorted and plunged yet faster through the forest which lay south of the capital. Normally it was foolhardy to gallop on the forest tracks, seamed with bony roots, especially toward the grove of Nemet.

Enda had traveled this very path two weeks before. The moon had been new; there had fallen only the light of the stars upon the darkness, upon the envy and loathing of the priests that must have twined around Enda like a suffocating shroud. Had Enda feared at all? No. No, Niall knew he had not, though in Enda's place he would have forsaken himself in abject fright. But he did not fear now, as he tore onward, with his sword at his side and his princehood around him like a mantle of impenetrable steel. Only the moon could make him afraid.

It was not far now. Even though the thick growth of the forest must swallow sound, they must be able to hear his horse's hooves ringing on the hard ground. Niall himself could hear nothing but that sound, and his horse's panting, and the desperate beat of his own blood in his ears.

He was right. They were waiting for him as he galloped into the grove, scattering turf cut by his gelding's hooves on their long, white robes. Within their circle he reined in sharply and slid to the ground, leaving his horse to jibe and kick, white-eyed, at the scent of ancient spilled blood. There was a noisomeness here that Niall could feel on his skin, like fetid swamp water. His hand on his sword, he looked around for Enda.

He had no chance. They closed in on him in fury, screaming curses against sacrilege. He fought, but they were so many, and they pressed so close upon him, that they soon disarmed him. All he could see was white, the dim shine of white robes in a forest clearing at night, and the pale hands that gripped him.

"Stand aside and let me see him," a cold, dry voice ordered.

Niall was jerked to his feet as the white robes parted. He faced a tall, old, grey-haired man, with pale blue eyes and long, knotted hands. Niall met his inimical gaze defiantly. "Archdruid Dralen," he said with cold courtesy.

No visible surprise touched the archdruid's face. "Prince," he said.

There was a murmur as the other druids recognized him. Niall raised one eyebrow as Dralen continued in silence. The old man understood. "Loose him," he commanded. "And restore to him his sword."

Free, Niall neglected to sheath his sword. Dralen correctly interpreted this oversight as insolence. "I want Enda Mac Mahon," Niall said. "Where is he?"

It was Dralen's turn to raise his brows. "An act of private vengeance, Prince? Surely you see that blasphemy must be punished before any other crime. The goddess must be satisfied."

"I have not come to cheat the Goddess of a victim—I mean, of a sacrifice," Niall lied smoothly. "I came to rescue a prophet. My prophet."

Niall ignored the renewed mutterings of the druids. Dralen's spine stiffened almost imperceptibly. "What foolish talk is this, Prince? It is we who prophesy for the kings. It is we who lead them, as well as the people, into correct observance of the gods' desires."

"No longer," Niall said easily. "At least, not entirely. What the gods intend for the people, they will receive. But a god has spoken to me.

"Four years ago, my lord Dralen, he threw us together, I a prince, he a shepherd. What were the odds against our meeting? Surely there was some reason beyond chance bringing us together. And that very first day, my lord, the god spoke to me through Enda. He entered Enda's flesh and used his voice, and he told me things neither I nor the shepherd knew. And in the years since then, the god has fostered our secret meetings.

"Each of us has grown increasingly certain of his will. Not long ago he spoke again, and told me clearly that Enda must and will serve me as my prophet when I become king. It was not an easy decision for either of us to accept, my lord." Niall paused, as artful as any tragedian of the Greek drama. "But we had no choice. When the gods speak, they brook no questions. What less than this imperative urgency could have driven me to Nemet this night? We must achieve the goals the gods set for us, my lord. Otherwise, we live and die in a darkness more fearful than any night can bring."

Niall had done. He knew that Dralen was not deceived by his lofty speech. It was clear to both of them that an incalculable political blow was being dealt to the druids. But it was also clear to both that Dralen could do nothing now to avert it. While the druids wore five colors, and the royals only four, there was no doubt which class the people loved better and looked to for leadership. Dralen did not dare harm Niall—not even by stealth, later—and without such a threat, was powerless to prevent his taking Enda away in safety.

But Niall had given the archdruid an out. Cleverly he had phrased his defiance in such terms as enabled Dralen to fashion a dignified submission to divine will from a loss of face. While the other druids were surely aware of what this submission actually betokened, they could maintain the polite fiction between themselves. Dralen lifted his hand.

"If this is true, Prince Niall, then as the Goddess's representative I tell you she graciously remits her vengeance in this case, in deference to her brother god, whichever god he may be. May the peasant serve you well as prophet." He did not trouble to keep disdain from his voice.

"Thank her for me," Niall said, deliberately infusing a delicate blend of irony and humility in his voice. "And now, where is Enda?"

"Go get him." Dralen jerked his head at two men who belonged to the hereditary class of druid's servants. They were the only laymen permitted to witness druid secrets without suffering death—by such means as made death, when at last it came, welcome.

149

Niall waited in silence as the two slaves disappeared into the forest edging the glade. The congregation of druids drew apart from him, so that he stood alone in the center of the grove, near a standing stone. He felt something from the stone, something that made him uneasy in the pit of his belly. He moved aside from it, ignoring the low laugh that came from the cluster of white robes at the edge of the clearing as he did so.

And as he stood there, waiting, sword now sheathed, his arms folded, the moon came up over the trees.

Niall's horse, quiet now, tethered at the edge of the clearing, lifted his head, ears pricked. Then Niall heard the rustle of footsteps through leaf litter. From the forest emerged the two slaves, with Enda held tight between them.

Niall had hardly thought how Enda might look. He was shocked, then his face went dark with anger. The shepherd was filthy and gaunt, his poor tunic torn, his canvas sandals gone. His feet were bloody, his hands cut and scabbed. His hair, matted with dirt, showed only a dull gleam of red. Fresh bruises purpled his white skin over older, yellowing marks. His wrists and ankles bore the burn of ropes.

Enda stumbled as he entered the grove. He looked upward, mesmerized, at the cold disc of moon, as if bewitched, a bird waiting for a snake to strike. He flinched as Niall took him gently by the arms. "Enda," the prince said softly, "it's me. Don't worry. You're safe now. Do you hear me? The moon can rot in the sky for all we care. Nothing will hurt you now."

The pity in Niall's voice got through to Enda as nothing else could have done. He straightened, and something came back into his eyes. For all his dishevelment he looked proud, and even kingly, the jutting bones of his starved face upholding a naked grandeur. The spirit that explained the god's choice of him had never shown more plainly than when he looked at Niall and said, curtly, but kindly: "You took your time."

Niall was taken aback; then he chuckled quietly, glancing at the moon. "We did leave it late, didn't we? Do you think you can sit my horse?"

Enda grinned. "Even if it kills me. Anything's better than going belly down across your saddle, kicking like a kidnapped virgin."

Niall had signaled wordlessly for his horse. A slave brought it, and remained holding the bridle while Niall himself gave a hand up to Enda. Stiffly, his face white with effort, or pain, Enda got up behind the saddle. He made no sound. Niall looked at his hands. They were stained with Enda's blood.

Say nothing, Niall clearly heard. You will have your hands full with their attempts to undermine you as it is. It is the people who will suffer if you vent your anger now.

Niall looked up quickly. Enda stared back at him blandly. "Get on the horse," he said softly.

Niall vaulted into the saddle as lightly as a zephyr. Enda, not too proud to realize he would fall off otherwise, hooked his arms around Niall's waist. Without a word to the huddle of white robes, Niall wheeled his gelding and galloped from Nemet.

The hoofbeats lost themselves in the darker echoes of the forest. The druids stood motionless and dumb in the grove, in the full light of their demanding and unpacified moon.

Niall did not ride straight back to the palace. Not thinking, acting on urges deeper than thought, he gave the capital a wide berth and rode on to the north. Enda, clinging, was lulled by the horse's smooth gait and his own exhaustion into a kind of trance. He noticed and cared nothing for their destination until the chilly air and their sudden lack of movement roused him.

Oddly enough, Enda had never before been here at night. It was so quiet that he fancied he could hear the bubbling of the spring as it welled into the hollowed white stone.

"Why did we come here?" he asked, as he slumped against the strong trunk of the oak.

Niall was taking a napkin full of raisins and dried venison, and a flask of wine, from his saddlebag. "I don't know," he answered. "It just seemed the only place to go. Eat this, and drink the wine. You look half dead."

Enda said nothing. He could not eat at first, but after a few swallows the good wine ran warmly through him, easing his body and making it possible, then delightful, to devour Niall's leftover marching rations. When the napkin was empty Niall took it from Enda's lap.

The shepherd—former shepherd, now by necessity prince's prophet, having nowhere to go except to Niall's protection—leaned back against the tree, eyes closed. His discolored face, pale as the moon pouring light from above, had grown compelling, with a strange, subtle virility unveiled by the fleeing of the last of childhood. Here-again-was a man to be heeded by anyone in whom stirred the frailest sense of overmastering verity, quietly unregarding of tangible proof, but real for all that.

Enda suddenly felt a lovely, healing coolness on his face. Niall had dipped the napkin into the spring and laid it on Enda's bruises. Enda did not move. Niall removed the cloth and repeated the laving on all of Enda's wounds, his torn hands and feet. The water seemed to tingle slightly on his injuries, as if these absorbed some property of it into him. The pain faded, dissipated, receded into a blur of harmless memory.

Enda sighed and opened his eyes. Niall was sitting crosslegged, watching him, his dark eyes unreadable in the shadow. Yet Enda knew. He reached out his hand. Niall extended his own. They touched, and tightened their grip, the one with the utmost confidence, the other with exultant peace.

Of course, the famous singer visiting the court of Meath composed a poem about the prince Niall and the shepherd Enda, when their story was made known. He sang of their boyhood meeting, when the god spoke through Enda to Niall; of their years of secret companionship; of Niall's rescue of Enda from Nemet, and the courage each had displayed. He sang of their friendship, forged by the gods themselves, which even the gods were powerless to destroy.

But of the white stone he did not sing, nor of its mysterious keeper, who had shown them so much. For the truth has a way of protecting itself from those not ready to know; and likewise, a way of breaking down all walls of unwillingness when the unready are so no longer.

And everywhere the poet travelled the people asked for the tale of the prince and the shepherd; and they did not need his solemn vow of witness, for in their hearts they knew that all they heard was true.

Thanks to

Lois Meneely O'Brien
Neil H. O'Brien
Ginny Long
George W. Fisk
John White

Giving thanks is the best part of receiving favors.